"Spiritual and all resplendent; it features talking beasts with magical gifts and deities who are reflective of the gods of known parables..."

— *Foreword* Clarion Reviews ★ ★ ★ ★

"A tale for our times, *The Once Upon a Time of Now* returns our attention to the gifts of this life: friendship and curiosity, creativity and wonder. Punctuated by timely breathing practices and original meditations, introducing deities and complex philosophical concepts in a lyrical, accessible way, this book is here to open your eyes and warm your heart."

— Elena Brower, bestselling author of *Practice You, Being You and Softening Time*

"...Luxuriate in the poetic language. Allow yourself to be intellectually stimulated... [*The Once Upon a Time of Now*] tenderly charts the myriad possibilities of our human condition..."

— Subashini Ganesan-Forbes,
Oregon Arts Commissioner,
former Portland Oregon Creative Laureate,
executive director of New Expressive Works

" ...Both Agnes and the reader come to appreciate the many treasures that can be found by looking within... Playfully immersive, the tale has much to teach."

— *Kirkus Reviews*

"*The Once Upon a Time of Now* is an homage to Indian culture, stories, and philosophy. An irresistible tale of life... to awaken curiosity and wonder... Hard to put it down!"

— Indu Arora, author of
Soma: 100 Heritage Recipes for Self-Care, Yoga: Ancient Heritage Tomorrow's Vision and Mudra: The Sacred Secret

"...The spirit of *Winnie the Pooh, Alice in Wonderland* and *The Chronicles of Narnia* meets Indian mythology resulting in an unlikely fusion that showcases profound spiritual wisdom... Full of playful winks to Indian philosophy, *The Once Upon a Time of Now* is a delight for connoisseurs of the subject and those hesitating on the threshold alike.

— Tova Olsson, author of
Yoga and Tantra- its history, philosophy and mythology

the once upon a time of now

mythic adventures, discoveries & meditations
in the forest of consciousness

hope west

smalltempleprojects

2023

◆ FriesenPress

One Printers Way
Altona, MB R0G 0B0
Canada

www.friesenpress.com

ISBN
978-1-03-916789-6 (Hardcover)
978-1-03-916788-9 (Paperback)
978-1-03-916790-2 (eBook)

1. Fiction, Visionary & Metaphysical

Distributed to the trade by The Ingram Book Company

to sleep on a story, always . . .

for

Momma

Nanny + Popeye

and Bhud, my very own Ji

contents

waxing half moon

waxing gibbous

full moon

. . . aum . . .

the beginning before the beginning

the end after the end

acknowledgements

This book is a love letter to the enormous generosity and depth of scholarship of my teacher, Dr. Douglas Renfrew Brooks, to the sweet, open-hearted erudition of his teacher, Dr. Gopala Sundaramoorty (Appa), and to the community of great hearts who form the Rajanaka Kula, past and present. Most of all, though, this book is a valentine to the people of India, whose enduring repository of mythic tales has no peer.

A wellspring of collected memories, Indian mythology offers an incomparably vast and sophisticated body of resources regarding what it means to be human, as well as what it *might* mean—our experiences, as well as our possibilities. To my mind there is no cultural treasure greater than the story traditions of India, and it has been my honour and delight to dive into this sea of myth, first through the academic study of its philosophies and iconography, then by exploring its experiential complexities as a practitioner.

This book is not an attempt to retell the legends of the gods; many are more qualified to do so than I. Instead, this tale is based on my own story of encountering these glorious deities and the enhanced meaning that cultivating a relationship with them has brought into my life. Told as a journey, it is dedicated to the idea of the "Long Way Home," a scenic route that invests in time and the appreciation of interpretation. Seeding our imagination, the Long Way ensures that a riot of wildflowers blossoms alongside every path we travel, that the air is always redolent, that the friends we meet along our journey are many, that the currency we spend is our attention.

Stories love to be told, and I have been fortunate to have been told many. My earliest memories are of snuggling next to my mum or one of my grandparents at bedtime, sent off to dream my own stories on the fantasies of another. In this way—this sharing of stories—culture creates and recreates itself, building on the memories of the past and ferrying those precious tales across oceans of time on the lips of myriad storytellers.

Constructed by humanity of human concerns, I have been taught that the gods are us and that we approach them all through our own lens, winnowing with our hearts and minds their complex worlds of existence. As such, I keep the focus on what I heard, not on what might have been said. So, this story is in no way meant to be an exhaustive description of the deities; instead, it relates simply facets of their very intricate characters. In addition, I have invented and added beings not part of the Hindu pantheon who nonetheless remain informed by the underpinnings of the philosophies I have studied.

No doubt, by straying too far from their idea of these divine energies, I will disappoint some. But India's most treasured offering is allowing for the vastness of individual analysis. Through our histories, our imaginations, and our circumstances we each establish our own connections to the 330 million gods—our experience, always our own. Still, it is my hope that my playful interpretations consistently convey the profound respect I hold for these mythic traditions.

My teacher and his teacher describe the gods as both mirror and prism: we see ourselves, and we see our possibilities. For me, these mythologies cracked open a universe of explorations of how to live my best life, not to focus on seeking answers (or "the" answer!) but instead to raise the stakes, enabling me to ask better questions. To hone my awareness. To allow the ordinary to become transcendent. To alter my vantage point. And perhaps most potently of all, to always keep good company, in mind, body, and heart. These myths remind me that to surround myself with greatness—in books, in food, in friendship, in music, in conversation, in art—is the surest route to expose my own creative potential.

Fostered by my love of the interpretation of myth and symbol, *The Once Upon a Time of Now* is a lighthearted allegorical inquiry into philosophical territory, with plenty of room for reflection. We set off on a journey where simple kindnesses buoy spirits and a shared goal forges enduring bonds, a pilgrimage where creativity is the progeny of the marriage of curiosity to commitment. You'll find practices to encourage your own dreamtime and to open a communication with the internal resources we name "the deities," allowing this adventure to become your adventure.

ACKNOWLEDGEMENTS

Indian mythology taught me to create a life I love. I have, and I do. And I hope you do too. So, please take the Long Way Home, and don't forget to stop and enjoy a sandwich along the way.

Ever,

Hope

XIV

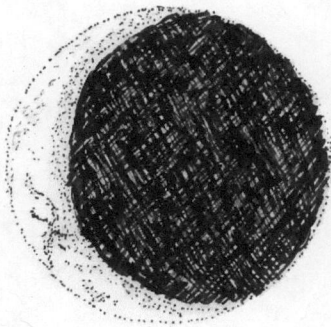

waning crescent

I

magic

"The world is full of magic things,
patiently waiting for our senses to grow sharper."

- W. B. YEATS

magic

One frosty night, a little Canadian girl marvelled at the moon and the myriad stars. The Big Dipper shone its cosmic question mark, bright in the winter sky.

"What's it all about . . .?" she mused.

Gently rocking to and fro, to and fro, the little girl perched on a swing in the park near her house, committing to the silence and the darkness of the north country's early December evening. From the immense sky above, a sense of wonder rained down, saturating her.

The world is just so big.

Regal Douglas Firs towered at the park's periphery, and like a cupped palm, the crescent moon floated even higher. Far into the beyond, the Milky Way softly flashed its own eternal presence. Agnes—for that was her name—leaned her head back, squinting up into the star-stippled sky. Today's math class had been about infinity, and the whole idea of its boundlessness had her mind all tangled up.

She rubbed a tired eye, but one shimmering speck in the distance continued to move uncertainly. Her forehead furrowed. Her head tilted. Agnes struggled to bring the light into focus. But the sparkle bobbed and weaved, bumped and lifted.

She stilled the swing. A shooting star . . .? Naaah. Too slow, too random. Instead of a straight line, the glow zigzagged a lazy undulation, as if searching for something . . . for someone.

Closer and closer it wobbled and quivered, until the light mote seemed almost reachable. Like a dream ghosting her consciousness, it dropped suddenly to the ground in front of her. She rubbed her eyes again, this time in disbelief. Shaking her head, she looked around.

The park was empty.

Yet there it was, right in front of the tetherball stand: a luminous . . . a luminous . . . well, a luminous something.

The small glow throbbed. Of course, she couldn't resist! Cautiously, she approached, stuck out a toe, and nudged it ever so gently. Seemed okay. Hunkering down, she examined it closely.

"Pfffft!" She laughed. "It's only a balloon!" But what was the source of its light? She picked it up, turning it over and over in her hands.

Strangely decorated, it was covered in esoteric symbols and—

"OUCH!!" she yelped, dropping the balloon quickly before realizing that from its string dangled a sharply curved pin.

She laughed again. She'd only pricked herself.

"Hmmmph!" Her oversized curiosity was delightfully aroused. And so, balloon in hand, the little girl hurried home, slamming the front door with a perfunctory "I'm baaaack!" to appease Momma, then took the stairs two at a time up to her room.

"Look!" she whispered loudly once the door to her bedroom clicked shut. "Look what I found in the park—or rather—what found me!"

She shared the mysterious arrival story (minus the slightly embarrassing self-induced pinprick) with the stuffed elephant on her bed. He lifted one large pink ear in interest as Agnes plopped onto the bed beside him.

"What do you think, G?" She handed him the balloon.

Crinkling his wide brow, G caressed its surface.

"Well?" she asked impatiently. "Whaddya think?"

"I thiinnkk . . ." G drawled sonorously, "that you should remember to e-nun-ci-ate."

Agnes blushed. "Okay, okay. Sorry! But what do you think, G? What should we do?"

"That my dear, well, that is as obvious as the trunk on my face. Use the pin! Pop the balloon!"

Agnes grinned, and without waiting, without arguing, without further ado of any kind, she pulled the pin from the string and poked the balloon—hard!

"The Big Bang!" G joked as the orb exploded. They both giggled.

"HOLY SMOKE! Check it out, G!" Agnes stage whispered as they stared at the mess on her bed. Bits of balloonery spread out here and there, but in their midst lay a tiny spiral of yellowed paper. G sucked in a loud breath. Agnes reached for the paper, and they knocked heads, both trying to get a closer look.

"We need Big Eye!" Agnes proclaimed, pulling open her bedside drawer to grab a large magnifying glass. Leaning in, they conked heads again. With nary a word, each absent-mindedly rubbing a slightly bruised noggin, they scrutinized the tight, ornate script and odd markings.

"A map?" Agnes proposed.

"Indeed." G nodded.

"An ancient map," Agnes expounded, "and . . . a brand-new mystery!"

Lifting his fuzzy pink eyebrows, G agreed. "Definitely!"

Without postmark, without authorship, floating on the winds for no one knows how long on its journey to the home of the little Canadian girl, this mysterious map could not have found a more worthy recipient. Small in stature— although taller than her sister—Agnes was possessed of extraordinarily keen observation skills and a fine mind, in addition to her immense curiosity. Together, she and her preternaturally calm, stuffed friend G would certainly bring a formidable focus to discerning just what the heck was going on here.

So, our story begins.

But be forewarned! A map may result in a translocation from A to B, but a story has the power to move one a boundless distance intellectually, psychologically, and emotionally while never yielding an inch in space. For as vast as your idea of the world is, the world of ideas is far vaster.

A million questions pulsed, but Agnes would have to slow her heartbeat and summon patience as Momma yelled out, "Bedtime!" Agnes and G dove under the covers in response. They would have to wait until morning for the next chapter of this mystery to unfold.

Sleep did not come easily that night for the little Canadian girl—nothing new. She generally had so many questions on her mind that the nighttime hours were spent thinking this and that, then this all over again. Of course, later, she circled right back to that.

Tonight, her thoughts were with the ancient map and how to solve the mystery of its arrival. What did it all have to do with her? Where would the map lead? The only answer she felt sure of was who would help her: G, of course. And knowing that he was the most perfect of companions with whom to enter into such an adventure as this (or any other!), she cuddled deeper under her quilt and finally, finally, finally, fell fast asleep.

2

beginning

"The clearest way into the universe
is through a forest wilderness."

- JOHN MUIR

beginning

Thus began their great adventure—or so they thought. However, aren't we always in the middle of the story? With a beginning before the beginning, an end after the end? That may well be the case, but for Agnes and G, this old map designated a very special moment, a very particular moment—it marked *this* moment. This *now*.

So, with curiosity and confidence, they prepared. Eyes and thoughts keenly focused. Many, many questions at the ready. With each other's total and unconditional support. And with voluminous pockets chock-full of Often-Quite-Handy items, Really-Good-Luck charms, and Can't-Leave-Home-Without-Its. Full of Don't-Forget thises and We-Might-Need thats, and of course, copious amounts of tempting, utterly necessary, and equally irresistible snacks.

Early the next morning, the air freshened by the unfailing northwest rain, hand in hand, the little Canadian girl and the fuzzy stuffed elephant made their way back to the neighbourhood park. It seemed the best place to unravel the trail, they'd decided, at just the very spot where the mystery itself had been initiated.

Once they arrived, though, the park looked just like the park on any other morning—teeming with kids and moms, perambulators and backpacks, picnic lunches and favoured toys—and absolutely no sense of anything out of the ordinary. Not at all.

"That's weird!" Agnes grumbled. The very ordinariness of it made this day seem all kinds of strange.

"I always find magic well camouflaged within the mundane," G reassured. "We just have to open ourselves to all the possibilities."

Agnes agreed. "Okay. Good plan." She chewed a bit on her lip, finally asking, "Where do you think we should start?"

G squinted his button eyes thoughtfully. Looked left, then right. Flapped furry pink ears. With consideration then, he offered his suggestion. "Shall we begin with a slide? Just to get the juices flowing?" G himself thought this a rather wise approach. He loved the slide—and when you don't know where you're going, why not start with what you love?

Agnes too loved the slide and nodded her appreciation of this exceptional idea. Up, up they climbed. Then down, down its serpentine route they went, ecstatic in their weightlessness and their speed as they twisted its length. Singing delight wide into the wintery air as they descended, the pair shrieked a wild and simultaneous "WHEEEEEEEEeee . . .!"

But at the end of the slide, there was no thudding re-entry upon a familiar mound of sand. None of the common-place playground sounds—the laughter, the squeals, the cajoling—greeted them as they thumped their way off. Everything they recognized, everything known, had completely vanished—even the playground itself was gone!

No swings, no tree house, no teeter-totter.

No kids, no moms, no backpacks—not even the very slide they'd just come zipping down. Everything around them had changed.

Agnes spoke first. "Where ARE we?!"

Greenery surrounded them, but these weren't the park's usual firs and pines. Instead, large glossy leaves bowed low over their heads, dappling the forest floor. The icy air had turned heavy and humid, and from the branches above, fat drops of dampness dripped in loud splats. Waves of heat blurred up from the ground…and the insects buzzing by their heads were HUGE!

"YIKES!!!" Agnes squealed, swatting at something particularly monstrous. "What the . . .?!"

G looked around—well, mostly, he looked up. Flat on his back where he had landed, the stuffing literally knocked right out of him, his huge ears were ringing disconcertedly and—even though it was daylight—G was pretty sure he was seeing stars. *This was completely discombobulating!*

Reaching up, he realized the problem: where was his head? This was not simply an expression. The fall had fully separated his head from his body. *Good grief!* With a pull both swift and sure, G reached for it and set it back onto his shoulders. "Uuuuugh . . ." he moaned, struggling to sit upright. "Forget about WHERE w-w-we are," he stuttered, his usual aplomb knocked out with his stuffing. "Look-look-look at me!"

Agnes drew a strong breath and whistled. "HOLY SMOKE, G! Whaddya think of that?!"

Out of long habit, G frowned, "Agnes, please e-nun-ci-ate!"

"Sure. Sure," she repeated. "But wow, G! Just WOW! Your head is a REAL elephant head! And you've got legs like a boy!"

Lifting himself onto his feet, G stretched his real elephant trunk in a big grey curl toward Agnes. She rubbed its soft skin. Real elephant eyes met little Canadian girl eyes, and they both grinned widely. This was turning into a very great adventure, indeed!

"G'day!"

Quickly, Agnes and G reached for each other's hands. Who had spoken?

"Hallo-hallo-hallo!"

Agnes looked to G, who lifted real elephant eyebrows and shook real elephant ears.

"Felicitations!" came the clipped tones of a heavy accent. The disembodied voice continued. "A terribly hard fall, what?! Bloody hell! Are you both okay?" The voice got louder and louder until it fairly yelled. "Did the tumble damage your ears? Can. You. Not. Hear. Me?"

Still uncertain, Agnes and G looked to each side, spun right around, then spun forward again.

"I'm here . . . Right up here! Up-up-up! Never mind," the voice finally sighed with resignation. "I'll just come down." And silent as a cat (!!), from the branches above, a glorious tiger leapt to the ground and landed right in front of them. Startled, Agnes and G fell backward, and more than a bit scared, they scuffled and scuttled awkwardly to regain their footing, still gripping each other's hands tightly.

"What ho!" sing-songed the tiger.

"Hello . . ." Agnes offered back hesitantly, her Canadian politeness more a habit than a willed choice.

"Why yes . . . Of course, of course, hello!" G echoed. Never having conversed with two hundred kilos of wild feline before, both young adventurers were somewhat perplexed.

"Jolly good!" The tiger's head tipped and bobbled from side to side. "Tiptop then?" he inquired in his jaunty musical English. "No doubt you've had a journey, and I'm chuffed to hear all about it. Fact is, I've had rather a bit of a peregrination myself, arriving here. Quite odd. Yes, indeed, quite odd," he repeated, striped head wagging. Stunned, Agnes and G stared back in silence.

"I have no idea of the time, but I wouldn't say nay to a spot of elevenses. Am I right?" the Bengal tiger asked. "You could tell me your plans. Explain where we are." Lifting his elegant nose, he pointed toward a comfortable area at the base of a nearby tree.

G readily agreed. "I am a bit peckish myself!" he admitted.

At this, Agnes smiled, knowing G was almost always ready to eat. "We're very happy to chat. Though I'm afraid we don't actually know where we are, sir." She glanced to G for confirmation. "As you saw, we've only just arrived ourselves, and, well . . . we were hoping you knew this place." G nodded solemnly.

"I?!" The tiger lifted dignified eyebrows. Stripes zigzagged as he shook his head with vigour. "N-No. Oh-no-no-no. Not I," he stammered his surprise. "I just dropped by . . . well, dropped in," he corrected himself. "Made a jump on my home turf. A lovely jump. A cracking jump! Very, very precise," he emphasized. "Took aim. Diamond clear as a thunderbolt. Jumped . . . then, ZZZZAPP! I was here." He yawned his wide jaw disconcertingly. "Shocking. So, no, haven't a clue. Haven't a clue. No-no-no-no-no-no. Not a one. Nope."

G looked at Agnes. Agnes looked at G.

"The whole confounded event has made me frightfully… well…don't suppose you've brought along any comestibles? A tasty tidbit or two?" A rosy tongue slathered ample tiger lips. "A delectable delicacy?"

Agnes grinned and knew just what to do next, plunging her small hand deep into oversized pockets.

Meeting the tiger, then, proved less an answer than a deepening of the mystery. Some days are just like that.

Nonetheless, two heads are better than one—as G became fond of saying—so no doubt three would be a notable improvement. And to enjoy a meal with a tiger? Well, that was just about the best beginning to an adventure Agnes could imagine! Settling themselves on a pile of leaves, the new friends discussed their current situation and just what to do next, crunching and munching contentedly.

3

memory

"Myth is never a single story.
It is always a tree with many branches."

– ROBERTO CALASSO

memory

Snacks over, the large cat groomed his resplendent whiskers. G dozed. Agnes wandered about, poking her inquisitive nose into their surroundings. What might she find just close by? The forest dripped and buzzed, trilled and swished, as bugs and birds and small slithering lives moved through its embellished thickness. From her voluminous skirt pockets, Agnes pulled Big Eye and lost herself in examination. The transparency of a celadon frog held her rapt. Then the spotted fur cloak of a humongous moth mesmerized. Hunkering low, she stilled to witness the scurrying exodus of a longlonglonglonglong trail of ants, toting the debris of the forest atop their diminutive bodies.

A rather large spider ambled up the delicate curl of a leaf, stopping directly beneath Agnes's magnifying glass. Agnes smiled—many might scream, but she rather liked spiders.

The spider lifted her head. Agnes gasped. Had this pretty spider just winked at her?!

Tinkling laughter filled the forest like so many bells. "I am the Holder of String," the spider said, introducing herself, "for I am both messenger and message. The Keeper of Tales, the Teller of Tales—I am the caretaker of what belongs to us all. You may call me Bhu."

Recovering her composure, as well as her manners, the little Canadian girl shared, "I am Agnes. I've come to this place with some friends."

"Oh yes, yes, I know," the charming spider replied. "The Earth is my ear. Who is here? Why have they come? All this is my business, as it is I who will repeat their stories."

"You know why we're here?!" Excited, Agnes got right to the point. "Please do tell me! Actually...." She hesitated in the embarrassment of the completeness of her ignorance. "I don't even know where—or exactly WHAT—here IS!"

Did the spider grow or did Agnes get smaller? Who knows? And does it really matter? For they now stood together under the trees, the spider and the young girl, both dwarfed under the immensity of the forest canopy.

"Sit, sit!" Bhu graciously waved her eight limbs, encouraging Agnes to settle in her lap. "Are you cozy?" she asked, and with Agnes's happy nod, she began her telling. For when she is asked—she always waits until asked—the Holder of String initiates a slight tug, a gentle pull on the twisted strands she carries within. Unravelling these tangles like an untold secret, she weaves a sparkling cloth of the three worlds: that which has Past, this very Now, all the possibilities of the Future. Bard as well as chronicler, the spider's tessellating tapestry creates warp and weft from what has been forgotten, embroidering it with what will be remembered. Out of the All Time, she spins her stories until—as curled as an ouroboros—they encircle themselves, melding into infinity.

However, the comely spider did not immediately speak. Instead, she simply listened. Shrouded in the sounds of the forest, Agnes listened too. Heaving SPLATs dropped... leaves rustled like fancy ball gowns . . . tiny chirps hiccupped, and ponderous creaks thwacked . . . splintered . . . busyness hummed attentively as all the green things grew.

In fact, it was surprisingly loud—louder than Agnes had ever realized "silence" could be!

The spider continued to listen, so the little girl did as well. Agnes listened so long and so intently that she heard her own breath fogging in the thick humidity, its very rhythm coordinating with the forest's pulsation. The extravagant foliage and the ruddy newts and the shy mouse nestling against the tree roots—even the Teller of Tales herself—breathed with one shared breath. Agnes's senses expanded, encompassing the myriad lives around her, and it was only then that the Holder of String was ready to recount her story.

The spider knew well that to listen is to connect.

With multiple eyes gazing back through time, Bhu dipped into an oceanic repository of knowledge . . . of ideas. She explored the width of all experiences to weave her tale anew. From her mind's darkest corners, she sought the shimmering, unsteady light from which to craft her narrative, walking in the skin of others. She sobbed their grief. Her heart thumped with the agitation of their joys. She absorbed their choices—those regretted as well as those celebrated. Emotions swam like swift waves over the storyteller's enchanting face.

"My telling is always distinctly my own," she explained, as the mirage of deep memory played across her face. "True, of course, of all we recollect. It is in the retelling that our imaginations inaugurate fresh connections, so that the stories remain alive. Indeed, stories love to be told!" This confession ignited her sparkling giggle.

Laughter hushed as the spider's voice transformed again to become many voices, colourfully flowing as she bridged here with there, then with now, this with that. Her conduit, rich with query and struggle, quivered in frustration and elation both. Eloquence formed a fabric of worlds plump with all those that had come before. She spun a collected history—a recollected history—of interpretation, understanding, inspiration. This, the abundance of her offering.

At last, the Teller of Tales recounted Agnes's own story, relating the night at the little girl's neighbourhood park and the discovery of the lighted balloon that fell to her feet from a dark night sky. "This cloth, this world—this is your story too, Agnes." The spider's silver laughter rang out.

"Will you hear it? Will you listen?" Bhu asked, as she retold Agnes's wonder, repeated all her perplexing questions.

The Holder of String untangled her thread, and Agnes travelled back, not simply remembering but—cradled in the spider's lap—again sensing all the feelings: awe, excitement, trepidation, astonishment. She and G planned again, packed again. Laughed heartily again too. How profoundly she cherished her G! And recognizing this, her trust in G's deep caring mirrored right back to her. The little Canadian girl's skin warmed in response to her feelings, wrapped in this blanket of goodwill—of friendship—until finally, the spider wove Agnes back into the present with her startling bump off the bottom of the slide.

Agnes sputtered at this time travel, this returning and recalling. "Why, yes! Yes—that's me! That's my story!" Honoured to know that she too was included in the repertoire of this glamourous Teller of Tales, Agnes's cheeks dimpled in delight.

"Indeed," the seductive spider smiled. "We are each a story, are we not? And who tells the tale first is a question that matters little, Agnes. Stories only truly live in their retelling. This is the giving of life—the giving of breath—to the tale. It is in the sharing that the recollection takes form, that it grows and becomes more through the reciprocity created in our imaginations. Each time we hear a story, *each time we share a story*, we invest a bit of ourselves in it. It becomes a part of us, so that in the midst of these retellings, we ourselves can live more fully. Generating networks—generating more of ourselves. Weaving a web of relationships."

The spider winked at her metaphor. "It is in this recollection that we find ourselves as many selves. We live realities that were never ours, times not our own, learn via the wisdom gathered by others. Living the life of a bee, we gather the nectar of our independent existences. And when we share that nectar—those experiences—honey is made. Only then is the sweetness of life fully enjoyed!" On cue, a fat bumble-bee blurred past Agnes's ear.

"These stories construct our memories and feed our dreams. I hold your story, as I hold all stories, Agnes. Woven into one exquisite fabric of experience, my many strings create the opportunity to live in the All Time—encountering this eternal now—where past and future constantly flow into every present moment."

Understanding surged in Agnes, and at this moment, in this now, Agnes promised herself that she would live the best story—the very best story—that she possibly could, envisioning her actions embroidered with all others into the shimmering fabric of the expansive universe.

Boldly, she questioned the spider. "You mention 'now,' which makes me think of 'here.' Perhaps you could tell me exactly where it is we have come."

"Ahhh!" Bhu exhaled slowly. "You and your G have made a mighty journey, Agnes. The tiger too. You have pierced the Theatre of Memory to arrive here in this Land of Light and Shadows." Majestically, she widened her limbs in every direction at once. As one might expect from one who lives to tell tales, the spider could be rather dramatic! "Here?" she announced grandly. "Why, this is the Forest of Consciousness!"

Agnes's eyebrows shot up, and her mouth opened in awe. She could barely contain herself. Monumental! "Wait till I tell the others!"

"Yes," agreed the spider soberly. "You have made a good beginning. But perhaps you can sense the forest's dappled light?"

Agnes looked about at the bespeckled forest. Clear sunshine made a jaunty bounce off shiny leaves, then fell rapidly into deep shade. Here, she could easily make out shapes and colours. There, all was lost in sombre gloom.

"You will find you have many, many challenges awaiting you, Agnes. Some dark times. Bitter disappointments. Perhaps sadness. Certainly frustration. Are you ready?" The little Canadian girl was always ready! Without hesitation, she jumped to her feet and nodded emphatically.

The Teller of Tales continued her warning. "You do have a rather large mystery to solve."

"HOLY SMOKE! I knew it!" Agnes yelped. "I knew there was a mystery! What is it? Please tell me!"

Smiling at the immensity of the enthusiasm spilling out of one small girl, Bhu acknowledged contentedly that a good story was definitely in the making. "The mystery you have come to solve . . ." She paused alluringly. Caught in the spider's web of suspense, Agnes leaned in expectantly.

"The mystery you have come to solve . . ." The Holder of String repeated, delighted to have this attentive (though decidedly limited) audience, she dragged out the fun. "The mystery is . . ."

27

Agnes barely breathed.

". . . To find the Lost Temple, of course!" the spider concluded.

It was Agnes's turn to repeat. "The Lost Temple?" Confused, she stammered out a trail of questions as longlonglonglonglong as the column of ants she had witnessed working so diligently. "What do you mean? Who loses a temple? How does one lose a temple? And where?"

"Well, that's why it's a mystery, Agnes!" the storyteller chided. "Be confident. As a great thinker of the past has quite aptly stated, all things excellent are as difficult as they are rare. He was really onto something! Remain diligent. Commit to your task. And do not get overwhelmed simply because it is all in front of you. Imagine if I were to start my spinning already considering the complexity of my task!"

The spider rolled her many eyes simultaneously. "You begin, Agnes. That is all. Then things happen. When they happen, consider your options. For me, perhaps a branch appears—I use it. Perhaps the wind destroys my work—I begin again. You make your choice in the moment you need to make it, with the resources you have at hand.

"Don't worry about what skills you might lack!" Bhu cautioned. "Once you begin, you will find that many will help you. Open yourself to their aid, Agnes. Use your community. This is how we flourish." Agnes thanked her, as the Teller of Tales prepared to take her leave.

"Inside me, I hold the exceptional—the treasure that belongs to us all. Yet remember, Agnes, as I have said, my tale is distinctly my own. Tell your own story, my

28

dear—always." And with this last bit of advice, the Holder of String nimbly traversed her leafy perch and disappeared into the undergrowth.

Was it illusion or truth that the spider had spoken?

"Yes," the forest answered. "Yes."

4
friendship

"Appreciation is a wonderful thing:
it makes what is excellent in others
belong to us as well."

- VOLTAIRE

friendship

Agnes made her way back to her friends. As she burst into the clearing, G and the tiger looked up expectantly. Smiling at her pals, Agnes quickly addressed the question in their eyes.

"I have good news and . . . well . . . slightly less good news . . . or maybe it's good news too," she stuttered.

"Good first!"

"Less good!"

Obviously, both friends had a slightly different philosophy when it came to hearing what might be heading their way.

"Less good!" repeated G. "I'd rather get the worst over with!"

"Good-good-good!" the big cat countered. "It will help prepare us for when things are less than tickety-boo!"

Agnes and G exchanged a nod, conceding that the tiger had a decent point there. Good it was, and good it would be.

"Well, I've just met someone who helped to explain where we are," she began.

"Whaaaaa??! Why didn't you say so?"

"Whaaaaa??! Why didn't you say so?"

Her friends erupted simultaneously, now both on exactly the same page.

"It's called the Forest of Consciousness." Agnes flopped down beside her friends, then launched in, doing her best to share what she had learned from the Teller of Tales. The tiger and G nodded, grimaced, shook their heads, and giggled nervously—it was a lot to take in.

"Annnnnd . . ." Emulating the spider's extravagant theatrics, Agnes stretched the single syllable before continuing. ". . . There's a great mystery to be solved!" Her voice rose as she topped up her report with whipped cream *and* a cherry.

G frowned suspiciously. "Wait! So, is this the good news or the not-so-good news?"

"Well, I guess it's both!" Agnes admitted. "It IS a mystery— A big one! And that's pretty cool, right?"

With this, G and the tiger had no argument. The three leaned back against the tree trunk, a bit sleepy from this long explanation, this new revelation, from the hodgepodge of thoughts and ideas and questions jumbling their minds. No doubt it was confusing, and they struggled to understand the implications, and that could be . . . well . . .

34

"Hahummm!" The tiger interrupted their musings. "I don't know about you two, but all this chin wagging has made me . . . hahumm . . . What do you say? Tiffin time, eh what? Any odds and sods left in your pockets, miss?" he inquired hopefully.

G's real elephant belly rumbled, and Agnes agreed—it had been an exhilarating morning and sustenance was called for. "Def-I-Nite-Ly!" she chimed, and back into her deep pockets she rummaged. Contentedly snacking their way through her findings, these fast friends concocted Big Important Plans.

"Okay." G's long trunk swung back and forth, wiping errant crumbs from his lap. "I've had a thought." Agnes and the tiger looked to the wisest among them with confidence.

"We'll mark this clearing as the centre," G began, "then walk in concentric circles out from here to see if we can find a path, an opening . . . anything that might give us a hint of the best route onward." At this, all three jumped to their feet, ready.

Agnes turned to the tiger. "You're a trained hunter." Haughtily, the tiger lifted his magnificent head a little higher. *My oh my,* he considered, *this little girl can state the obvious!*

"I am. I am, indeed," he concurred (con-purred?). "I'm jolly good—many might say top drawer, actually. Matchless, even. Unsurpassed and unequalled." Pride finally got the better of him as superlatives smoothed off his tongue in his sueded tones. "Unrivalled. Outstanding. Incomparable. Positively spiffing."

How long could this go on?! "Surely you have hints for us then?" Agnes asked, gently disrupting the grandstand.

G turned to the tiger. This was well asked. It's not only a sensible approach to solicit the advice of those with experience; it's flat-out brilliant.

The tiger considered the little girl's resourceful question, tilting his glorious striped head. Finally, in his clipped manner, he brusquely answered: "Pay attention!"

Then, on silent pads, he inaugurated their circuit through the trees.

G and Agnes looked at each other, grinned widely, and shrugged. Though a simple answer, it really was quite profound.

Sharpening their senses, sharpening their wits, they followed the big cat clockwise through the underbrush. The three spun and spun and spun, creating wider and wider circles, coiling their verdant corkscrew deeper, then deeper, into the forest. *Pay attention! Pay attention!* Their mantra reverberated as they looked for clues, for signs, for inklings of any kind. G moved lightly, despite his substantial girth, and his sensitive trunk sought any whiff of an intimation.

"Pay attention! Pay attention!" Agnes repeated to herself as she skipped over fallen branches.

"Pay attention! Pay attention!" she whispered as she knelt, scrutinizing the ground for evidence.

Tirelessly until twilight, the three carried on, expanding their circles, stopping only for snacks, then returning to spin and spin and spin their spiral. Though a distinguished travelling companion, the tiger—as all cats both large and small—often preferred his own company. He wandered ahead, paws hushed, eyes intent, dissolving like a shadow into the thick growth.

Returning in a flash, his wet nose trembled and his nostrils flared.

"I smell something. Or rather . . . SOMEONE!" he rumbled ominously. Their advance through the dense greenery abruptly halted, and Agnes and G fell in behind the tiger. *Pay attention! Pay attention!* They listened, stretching their senses into the umbrage, widening their aural net to snare the furthest sounds. Eyelids lowered, they squinted into the leafy shade. What didn't belong? Who was hiding . . . just out of sight? Little girl nostrils wrinkled and twitched as Agnes tried her utmost to meet the scent challenge the tiger had presented.

"ROARRRRRR!!!" It came from behind them: a sudden deafening discharge.

"ROARRRRRRRR!" The world around them shook uncertainly.

In an instant, the tiger leapt to confront the intruder and shield his friends. His striped head quivered in disbelief as he faced his own near-mirror image. A similar shiver echoed from an equally imposing, equally impressive—yet entirely spotted—head. Both cats frowned similarly lush, furry foreheads at this disrespectful mimicry. Both yawned comparably expansive jaws and exposed their many, many near-identical razor-sharp teeth.

"ROAAAAAR!!"

With corresponding ferocity, a simultaneous vocal explosion, the two cats rattled shiny leaves and shook curving branches, leaving Agnes and G splatter-smacked with forest dampness. Rivulets of moisture utterly drenched them as the little girl and the chubby elephant-headed boy stood stock still. Patience truly is a form of action.

This new cat, a lithe cheetah, bellowed in a mighty voice, "SPOTS!"

More fat drops from the branches above washed over Agnes and G.

The tiger lifted fuzzy brows at this incredible impertinence. What an affront! "STRIPES!" he thundered back, vehement in his self-satisfaction.

"SPOTS!" blustered the cheetah, with singular focus.

The tiger argued his case for pre-eminence. "Don't be daft! Dark ripples across the water—STRIPES!"

"The stars! The constellations! I am ChiChi. I sparkle like the very heavens above!" The dotted cheetah advanced his own exalted billing.

"SPOTS!"

"STRIPES!"

"SPOTS!"

At an impasse, the imposing felines each vociferously stood their ground. ChiChi was justifiably pleased with his lush, freckled coat. This conceit rubbed the elegant tiger the wrong way, and in his irritation, opulent striped fur stood on end. Their rivalry had brought the expedition to a standstill, and in the distance, the red flames of sunset lapped the sky.

"ENOUGH!" Exasperated by this relentless competition—this unnecessary shift from the importance of their mission—tiny Agnes boldly (foolishly?) walked between the cheetah and the tiger, admonishing them. "Haven't we all heard enough bickering in our lives to know that it solves nothing? Are our hearts not big enough to envelop more?

"You are both exquisite, and you both have every right to be pleased with yourselves. You are truly resplendent!" The little Canadian girl assuaged ruffled feelings, doing a right bang-up job of demonstrating her country's reputation for diplomacy.

For two cats, the tiger and the cheetah began to look pretty darn sheepish.

"Why not be proud of each other, as well?" Agnes suggested. "Wouldn't that double your enjoyment?"

The two felines pondered this possibility—as everyone knows, cats are invariably keen to enhance their own pleasure. Agnes recalled well the spider's instruction and deftly shared her understanding of it with the others.

"Is it not the greatest boon of friendship to expose ourselves to another's life?" Agnes asked. "To see through new eyes? To hear a different story? It's the best!" she exclaimed. "ChiChi, I invite you to join us on our quest. By knitting ourselves together—delighting in our shared successes, consoling each other when frustration mounts—we will certainly be expanded by each other's experience."

Driving the point home, she added, "There are so very many marvelous things to do that we can't possibly do them all! When we share our friends' experiences—when we share their feelings—why . . . it's almost like having the experience ourselves. And when I share with you, and you share with me, then it's even better!

"Each of you adds something wonderful to this group," she continued. "Something extraordinary. Something that only you can bring." It was not the roseate evening sky that tinted feline fur pink as the cats blushed at her compliments—and perhaps a little at their own silly squabble, so paltry a concern as they began a potentially glorious adventure.

Addressing the tiger directly, Agnes soothed, "Your stripes are indeed like dark ripples on water. But did you know they are also inky serpents, zigzagging the path? A bolt of lightning? A lonely horizon? Your family is well named a Streak of Tigers, as your black stripes convey shadowed messages of great speed—messages of brilliant clarity and intention." Calmed now, the tiger curled himself on the ground.

"From now on, let's call you Streak," Agnes suggested. G nodded. Contented, Streak dropped his striped head onto wide paws.

ChiChi looked trustingly to Agnes. "Is a group of cheetahs a ChiChi?"

"No." She laughed. "I am sure you are the one and only ChiChi! Your family, though, is distinguished as a Coalition of Cheetahs. A living consolidation of energy, your spots illustrate clusters of incredible power—potency itself—as aptitude and efficacy coalesce."

ChiChi padded over to Streak, nudged alongside him, and the two melted bonelessly into one another until no one could tell where stripes ended and spots began. Then— engaging in what cats do best when immersed in mutual appreciation—they licked one another's sumptuous fur coats.

"Your stripes really are quite spectacular," ChiChi murmured. Streak purrrrred.

"Well done, little one!" G whispered his approval. Agnes's heart raced from the passion of her speech—the recognition of the Holder of String's teaching in action—and well, it raced a bit too from her rashness in standing between those powerful cats.

Time for a good night's rest!

5
community

"If you aren't in over your head,
how do you know how tall you are?"

- T. S. ELIOT

community

Capitalizing on cooler temperatures, by dawn the forest was abuzz with activity. Creatures on the Night Shift returned home. The Day Shift began. With sleepy eyes still half-closed, Agnes watched as the scene around her quivered and shifted as bodies large and small wriggled and fluttered and scrabbled. Envious of their lazy liquidity, she squinted as the two big cats stretched their molten fur. She admired G, a moving meditation, describing fire and earth, air and water with his Qigong movements. A ruby dawn warmed the world.

Creeping her fingers down to the depth of her pockets, Agnes was disappointed; what fare remained within was meagre indeed. This morning, breakfast would be light. Still, no one complained as she doled out a share to each, a sunny smile on her face. Everyone chewed thoughtfully, prolonging the meal, hoping to make it feel like more. Perhaps it was just wishful thinking, but it seemed to work . . . kind of . . . at least for a while. Then one by one, rumblings could be heard from deep within bellies of all sizes and shapes.

"What's that?" Agnes lifted a finger to her lips. The group halted their last nibbles to listen. The sound of masticating continued. Clearly, someone had found something more substantial to eat. Cat eyes darted to elephant eyes to little girl eyes. It wasn't them!

"Chomp, chomp, slobber, SSSLURP!" All eyes widened at this very vocal enjoyment. Who was it?!

Little girl eyes lifted to cat eyes lifted to elephant eyes to—wait! Whose eyes were those waaaaaay up there?! All chins tilted up to view this extra set of brown eyes, bulbous and lethargically lidded. Surreptitious glances travelled down its neck . . . down its neck . . . down—Whaaaa . . .? That was some kind of long neck! Curious eyes moved along and along its seemingly endless span until they finally reached a body—and a conclusion.

"A giraffe!" they shouted as one. Drooping eyelids fluttered lazily, as the head on the elongated neck languidly turned.

"Where?" the giraffe drawled.

Agnes and G laughed out loud. "Why, it's you! Don't you know you're a giraffe?" Agnes asked with a grin, teasing their lanky newcomer.

Large lips slowly lifted into an easy smile. "Me?" he asked. "Well, no one's ever called me that before . . . but now that you mention it"—dark eyes melted down over his attenuated form— "I think you're right!"

With this they all chuckled heartily, including the giraffe, who then offered to share his ample breakfast. While his movements were slow, new friendships were rapidly made, and the considerate giraffe happily joined their pilgrimage. His steady good humour was easy to appreciate, as was his expertise at sussing out delicious vegetation. To this new companion, the forest was a seriously well-stocked pantry. His height added an instant advantage. And was it simply serendipitous that he glowed silver in the shadows, his iridescent coat helping to light their path? Some days, good luck brims your cup.

As the group readied to begin the day's trek, Agnes invited their statuesque friend to add to their reconnaissance. "Just what is it that you see?"

Fully extending his interminable neck, the giraffe pierced the scruffy lower canopy, his head disappearing into the upper leaves.

His muffled voice filtered back. "I can see the Lost Temple!" A cheer erupted. The giraffe dipped his neck back down, but as his head re-emerged, he tempered his findings: "Well, at least . . . I see the temple gateways. I'm sorry to say, though, that they're an awfully long way away."

The cheering stopped, and the giraffe sighed, his forehead corrugating with dismay in the delivery of this disheartening news. G though, was unfazed.

"It's okay," he reassured the friends. "The long way is always the most interesting way!" One by one, the companions nodded their agreement.

Seeking to comfort the giraffe, Agnes suggested a name for him. "Your ability is special. And it is proving invaluable—it's very helpful to know what's ahead. Besides," she laughed, "without you, we'd all be famished! Let's call you Finder." Pleased to be appreciated—and who isn't? —his burden eased, the giraffe stretched once again, his head vanishing back into the treetops as he returned to his fully telescoped height.

"The Temple walls are stone, thick, and precipitously high." In spite of this dire report, he bent back to his friends, his bright demeanour fully recovered as an extremely long, very wet tongue sloshed over large lips. Gleeful, he shared the good news: "Delectable-looking leaves up ahead!" And away he loped, leaving the travelling party scurrying to follow his elongated gait.

Flanked by her friends, the little Canadian girl felt her spirits loft on a mighty wave of gratitude. Steadfast and true, G, with his startling erudition and light heart; the illuminating giraffe, Finder, offering his wondrously expansive view; circumspect, valiant, and collaborative, the two cats, Streak and ChiChi . . . Agnes keenly recognized the value of always keeping good company. And on a journey such as this—into uncertain, perhaps even perilous territory—good company was unquestionably paramount. In her eyes, this gathering of great souls ensured that their enterprise was already a resounding success!

Slipping her tiny hand into G's, Agnes smiled contentedly as they trekked onward.

new moon

6

space

"Not only do we live among the stars,
the stars live within us."

- NEIL DEGRASSE TYSON

space

The companions lounged quietly, weary after their long day. It was a dark night, and the stars filled the sky with their breathtaking scintillation. All sighed at the miracle above.

Finder turned to G. "Will you tell us a story?" he asked.

"Yes! Yes! A story!" the big cats echoed, and Agnes beamed in anticipation. G always told the best stories!

More than happy to oblige his friends—after all, stories live to be told—G began.

Gesturing to the Milky Way, he asked, "Do you see this alabaster Serpent Queen above us?" he asked. "She spends all night in the sky, moving upon eternity, undulating her exquisite body to sparkle silently through the vast openness of space. Writhing her tail of cosmic dust, she entwines the wide-winged embrace of the Stellar Swan's summer migration." At this G pointed toward the Cygnus constellation, arcing the celestial flight of the astral swan.

Moving his finger to Orion, G continued. "The Serpent Queen wriggles across the Sky Dancer, enveloped in the perpetual beat of his drum—the heartbeat of the universe.

She ponders the abiding curiosity of the Seven Sages, as their celestial question mark continues its languid seasonal rotation." Here, from the powerful body of Ursa Major, he indicated the seven stars that form the Big Dipper.

"Across the inky vault of the heavens," G intoned, "the Serpent Queen sparkles her expansive silver river. Night after night after night, she unveils her spectral form, weaving its radiant wave resolutely through the skies. 'Why does she do this?' you might wonder. What buoys her spirits? Keeps her commitment strong? How does this milky one continuously nourish a dedication to her endless quest?"

At this, Agnes squirmed uncomfortably. Was G making a point here, speaking to her own propensity to tire quickly? To lose interest? Quite likely. Agnes made sure she listened closely.

"Certainly," G insisted, "it is this very query that the Seven Sages themselves pose again and again. Coalescing their light bodies in community, they broadcast their interrogation across the universe. 'Why...? Why...? Why...?' In spring, in summer, in autumn, in winter, together these seven stars twinkle their curiosity, sparking those who would take up their challenge to wonder along with them. What is the Serpent Queen looking for? Whom does she seek? As to what moves her, perhaps she herself best answers their inquiry." G looked at each of his friends in turn, holding their eyes for a moment before carrying on.

"For as with all those who truly seek—those who truly question—more than anything else, the Serpent Queen desires to look within. She yearns to reflect upon her own nature, her own motivation. She aches to know her propensities, to explore her capabilities, to manifest her own possibilities. And so, then . . . in the dark wonder of limitless space . . . in the immeasurableness of unending time, the Serpent Queen spirals back upon herself to locate her own milky tail. Widening her boundless mouth to receive it, she bands the Earth in her silver circle of infinitude."

In the silence of G's pause, the group scanned the river of stars gleaming in the heavens above them. It was a wide, wide world indeed.

G continued. "She seeks herself. She receives herself. She considers herself . . . and from that inner reflection, she illuminates all others, amplifying her own gifts by offering her sparkling nature to those who would listen . . . to those who themselves seek understanding."

G swivelled his large head to his friends. "Keep this in mind!" he urged. All eyes were held rapt.

"Of course, this Astral River is very, very old. Nearly as old as space itself. Nearly as old as eternity. She has witnessed the experiences of the All Time, so she has many, many tales to tell. In fact, the Serpent Queen has all the stories to tell because she herself is all remembrance, all thought, all attention. She is the Once Upon a Time of Now, and here is one of her tales:

"The Universe birthed a beautiful daughter, naming her Morning's Glory (though most everyone just called her Glory). One fall day, when Morning's Glory had grown to maidenhood, the air crisp-edged after summer's exuberance, a beautiful spider named Bhu knocked at their door and was invited to stay through the winter—a long and particularly chilly one."

Agnes smiled at the mention of one of her first extraordinary acquaintances of the forest. A tale of the Teller of Tales herself? This was exceptional! Arms wrapped tightly around legs as Agnes curled upon herself, mimicking the ouroboros of the Serpent Queen.

G continued his narration: "To keep their fingers nimble, hovering close to the fire, Bhu taught Morning's Glory to weave the scintillant threads unique to her people. Glory was an adept student, and by winter's end, the delicate fibres emerged from her slim fingers with ease. Strong and pliant, the prismatic threads danced in the light, and on even the softest breath, they were now visible, now disappearing, now visible again—as if by magic.

"Finally, the frosty weather abated. As a gentle spring breeze drifted through the cottage, the spider thanked the Universe for her hospitality and kissed Morning's Glory once on each cheek. Then leaning towards her, she whispered into the young girl's ear, speaking for a minute, maybe two, her muted voice tickling Glory's ear. Then stepping lightly upon one of her own ethereal fibres, Bhu floated through the open window and disappeared on an evanescent gust.

"Morning's Glory was so sorry to see Bhu leave! Like fat raindrops, tears splashed down her rosy cheeks. Still, she had heard the wondrous secret that the spider had shared. Clarity came to her. Nodding an understanding, Glory dried away her sadness and set to work.

"Once she appreciated Bhu's hidden truth, Glory was no longer satisfied to spin single threads; instead, she began to weave her brilliant skeins into a remarkable fabric. Each day her skill increased, her composition becoming more and more elaborate, dazzling the eye with its varied glimmering colours. She remained vexed, though, for as she held the spider's voice deep in her heart, listening carefully to its resonant echo, she felt she had not yet found its proper translation.

"Still Glory remained diligent. Staying the course, she worked deep into the night with only the flash of her fabric to light her loom. Till late one afternoon, as summer turned again to fall, and the goldenrod stretched bright heads to catch the last sunshine, Glory stared from her window at the lush beauty outside. Unfocused, she took in a broad peripheral view, her eyes open, her ears open, her heart open.

"In this spaciousness, Glory had a sudden thought—an epiphany, really. In order to create more widely, she had to experience more widely. Rather than attempting to evoke solely from within, she needed to be in conversation . . . listening to the wind pass through her as if through the limbs of a tree. She needed to welcome the origins of imagination and participate with the energies . . . all the beingness around her.

"With renewed enthusiasm, Glory hurried back to her loom and began to weave the azure of this late-summer sky with its gradual shift to twilight. Tipping her head thoughtfully, she wove in the robin's evening trill, the crows' guffaws as they gathered with their companions, and the buzziness of the bees, planning a sleepover in the bachelor buttons. Connecting with the fullness of the spider's tale, Morning's Glory wove her own longing for companionship—with those dearest to her heart, as well as with those she had never known.

"She wove the ribald songs of the milkmaids, their anklets tinkling as they passed the cottage on their way to the barns. She wove the petrichor of midday's heat as storm clouds greyed, the narcotic trail of roses, the lush press of moss underfoot . . . All this emerged from Glory's fingers as they flitted like dragonflies across her loom. One spindle found a moment fully savoured. Still another, the sacred act of a promise kept. Another, the preciousness of daydreams.

"As her tapestry grew and grew, Morning's Glory let the folds fall onto the cottage floor, let them flap happily out the door and up the chimney, let them zigzag out into the fields and ruffle the stillness of the lake. The folds swaddled wide tree trunks and high branches. Birds plucked at its loose threads to line their nests.

"The folds buoyed out exuberantly with the tide. Like a shared idea, they rippled across the sea. Floating, floating until—like fallen sails—they sank to the greatest benthic depths. At each shoreline, her cloth pleated in and out, in and out, breathing as the waves breathed. Its folds corrugated over mountains, spelunked into caverns, drifted up and down, over and under, until Glory's magical undulant tapestry wrapped the entire face of the Earth. Still, she loomed on . . . fiercely insistent, weaving the sublime energies into form.

"Pleasure and curiosity and murky shades of longing devised her weft. Wit and wisdom, source and cause, shaped the warp. Glory wove narratives of lives lived in joy and hope, in heroism, and loneliness, and the darkest of nightmares, each thin thread initiated by a moment—a choice made. When combined, the potential of both beauty and devastation increased, refracting colours and tone and redolence in the surrounding fabric. Each stitch, a particle distinct, yet each irrefragably—even indispensably—embedded into an environment, reflecting that environment, participating in that environment.

"Wonder and courage and unshakable melancholy. Everything valued and everything nurtured. Everything feared, every tolerance, every grey sadness. Morning's Glory continued each day to weave and weave and weave, until every magnificent memory, every heart's effort, every soul's story, every aching desire, every realization, every regret, every harmonizing voice, and every lamentation was present in the incandescent landscape of her cloth. Into her fabric, Glory wove every version of every tale of every history that the splendid spider had whispered into her ear.

"Her tapestry was a shelter, a ceremony . . . an iridescent fête. Every fibre shimmered with threads hinting of possible collaborations, braided portals of shadow and discovery, junctures of meaning, of pilgrimages not taken, of wars waged and those averted.

"Glory stayed committed to her task, until one day, the Universe inquired, 'What is it you are weaving, my dear?'

"'Oh, this is not really my creation, Momma,' Morning's Glory explained. 'I am retelling the stories Bhu shared with me before she left, the choices of all who live—and have ever lived—within you. Every decision made. Every eventual regret. Everything valued. Every past and present action, and every future hope. Thriving relationships. Egregious injustice. This cloth is all that. All connection. All relationship. It is grief, and it is truth. It forms the sea of the unknown, the sea of dreams. It is Memory's Cloth.'

"'Hmmm . . . lovely . . .' her mother drawled, a bit unconvincingly, wrinkling her brow at the vision of her shrouded Earth. 'It's getting rather large though, dear, don't you think?' she asked.

"'Yes, yes. I know, Momma. Do you have an idea where to keep it?' Glory smiled—knowing her mother always had an idea—then reached for a muffin. She hadn't eaten in forever, and she was starving!

"'Well . . .' The Universe considered. 'How about if I hang it in the heavens? They have a lot of . . . ummm . . . space.' She winked.

"'Mmphmmmf, Momma!' Glory munched (translation: 'Perfect, Momma!')

"She passed her mother the selvage, and with an immense burst of energy, the Universe cast it high into the expansive cosmos, draping it across the width of the horizon. Lifting their chins, the two deities admired the tapestry's twinkling nodes in the darkness. Great luminous rivers swirled across the skies as this Ocean of Starlight found its home.

"'You are making something exquisite, my dear,' the Universe sighed with admiration. 'Look how the lights create a pattern there—like a Sky Dancer, his arms raised in rhythm, suggesting the movement inherent in all that appears still!'

"'Thank you, Momma,' Glory mumbled, her mouth still full.

"'Oh! Oh! And look there!' The Universe pointed. 'A Great Bear! And a Swan!' she called out excitedly, finding shape after shape—the wholeness hidden behind difference—illuminating her night sky's former uniformity. Glory smiled as her mother clapped. 'It's as wonderful as a dream!'

"'A shared dream, Momma!' Glory popped another muffin into her mouth, delighted with this appreciation.

"'May I add Time?' the Universe asked.

"Glory smiled. 'Oh yes, please! I was really hoping that you would.' She loved this invention of her mother's.

"The Universe raised her left arm, sweeping it in a vast clockwise arc. Slowly, slowly, Glory's Celestial Ocean began to rotate, pivoting around one central light mote, which Glory named the Immovable. Rapt, the two watched as the Stellar Swan migrated, the Sky Dancer swayed, and the Seven Sages initiated their everlasting contemplation.

"'What do you call your material?' the Universe asked.

"'Call it...?' Morning's Glory munched. Apropos a goddess, she provided no answer, simply another question as she nibbled, her mouth full: 'Mmphffph matter?' ('Does it matter?')

"'Matter?' the Universe repeated. 'Oh my! Why, that's a lovely name! Quite perfect!'"

G concluded his tale: "And so, this then . . . was that." He looked around expectantly but saw that each of his friends had already fallen deeply asleep. Gazing back at the sky, G shrugged and smiled up at the undulatory Milky Way. Did the Serpent Queen return his smile? Well, no. But as befits starlight, she winked.

The next morning, Agnes awoke with her head nuzzled into G's arms. With perplexity, she reconsidered G's glamourous bedtime tale. She had been the one to meet Bhu, so how had G known a story about her? Stroking his smooth tusks until he too awoke, Agnes posited her question. G just laughed, his great belly shaking.

"Really, Agnes! You know better," he chuckled. "It's a story—not a history!"

True, she thought as they broke camp for the day's trail. Yet she knew her friend had undergone an immense transformation. Perhaps he too had met the pretty spider? He hadn't said he hadn't; he'd simply sidestepped her question. Something seemed fishy . . .

Like he wasn't really G. Yet he was.

Like G wasn't fully G. Yet he was.

Like G was G but more than G. Yes, that was it exactly! G was harbouring a secret—a substantial secret. What could it be? Though inordinately curious, Agnes trusted her old friend completely and was confident that, when the time was right, G would share what he was learning.

7

growth

"You enter the forest at the darkest point,
where there is no path."

- JOSEPH CAMPBELL

growth

Agnes looked up at her elephant-headed friend and admitted to her recent observation. "You know, I really do think you're growing, G."

ChiChi nodded.

"Yes, yes. Quite right!" Streak concurred.

G glanced expectantly at the giraffe, who lifted lanky shoulders, shook his head, and grinned. "Still look short to me!"

Agnes stepped up close to G, and putting a hand atop her own head, registered her fingers against G's chest.

"Oh my!" G grimaced at her marker. "I *have* grown. You know, I've been feeling a bit odd too," he admitted. "Not out of sorts, exactly. Just not myself. In some ways, I'm better— my thoughts clearer, my eyesight sharper. And actually, I can hear . . ."—he shimmied his capacious ears— "everything!"

Agnes was concerned. "We better keep a close eye on you." Still, each morning, under her watchful gaze, G's transformation continued.

A few days passed, till she woke one morning to find that G had disappeared. Had he just wandered off? The companions waited, of course. And worried.

When a full day and a full night passed, G had still not returned. They searched, their voices ringing into the forest until they were hoarse. But it seemed G was gone . . . at least for now.

So, they continued the journey. Streak lifted Agnes onto his back when she tired, trying his best to fill G's place, as they all did. Nonetheless, G's disappearance ripped a wide hole in their universe—as the loss of our very special people is wont to do. His wise, mirthful presence was much missed. Agnes suffered the loss stoically, yet she felt her own joy at their adventure diminish. Scanning the path from left to right for evidence, hunkering down with Big Eye, calling into the shadows—G remained ever in her heart. Constantly, she reminded Finder to lift his height above the canopy and search the distance for her old friend.

Late one afternoon, the group entered a lovely clearing and made camp. Finder loped off to fetch dinner. While the cats groomed each other, Agnes leaned her back against a large rock, letting her thoughts drift until her head nodded to her chest, and finally, she dozed.

A sonorous "Ahem!" startled her awake.

"G!" she sang out before his name caught in her throat. Confused, she squinted up, wondering, *Is this really my friend?* Of course not! The Great Being in front of her blocked the light with his girth, and although much about him seemed familiar, this being had four arms! Yet, he had an elephant head . . . a boy's body. *Could it be? Could it be?* Agnes repeated to herself.

Indeed, it was.

Her best friend had returned: enlarged, expanded, and now multi-armed. Formal, even archaic, in his speech, G bowed to greet Agnes with a thousand blessings. And while immensely relieved to find him again, Agnes sensed that things were definitely different. It was apparent that G had continued the remarkable transformation initiated with the beginning of their journey. His innate intelligence sparkled more brightly, and an incredible sweetness warmed his genial eyes. His laughter, still quick, was heartier. His step lighter, more graceful. Around G's broad waist—now as rounded as the full moon—twisted a serpent as black as the night sky. As wide as winnowing baskets, his ears flapped and twitched sensitively at even the slightest sound.

No. G was not the old G, and yet he still was—and more. Much more. Agnes threw herself into the multiple arms of her dear pal.

"What has happened, my G?" Agnes asked. "Where have you been? We searched and searched!"

G looked down with kindness at the little girl. "This Forest of Consciousness, Agnes, contains countless treasures for those who seek them. It's true I explored a different path—as you too, my dear, must continue to pursue your own way, even when that road undulates like the cobra of my belt. Even when the trail seems unconnected. For a path zigzags, and in order to find our own track, we must be willing to bend and move with it."

Agnes interrupted, "Oh no! G, you've been hurt!"

Indeed, one of G's tusks had broken, and Agnes reached for it with concern. The Great Being shook his large head and smiled encouragingly. "Don't worry, Agnes—I'm fine. It's actually a great story, and I'll tell you all about it one day. It's a perfect example, though, of how we must allow ourselves to fracture, just as sometimes our path disappears, splits, or even breaks. This is how we all develop. Occasionally we might lose our way—it happens. But if we trek on and stay true, we find the path again. My walkabout took me on a solo journey for a bit, but now I rejoin you and our fine companions."

Agnes clapped her hands as G continued. "Together, we will persevere on our shared quest."

"Oh, I'm so glad you're back!" Agnes threw herself again into G's many arms and hugged tight. "I've missed you so! But I knew you'd return—I just knew it." Her curiosity got the better of her as she blurted out a whirlwind of questions: "Where exactly did you go? What did you see? Who did you meet? Will you share with me a little of what you experienced, G?"

Amused, G lifted a hand, and she stopped to listen intently to his response: "In my transformation, I travelled from now to then, widening my vision. My hearing was honed as I moved from this to that. And by exploring the liminal space between here and there, I found that the best answer is always to pose a better question!"

He explained further. "By inviting the opportunities that appear between boundaries, we develop our shifting skills. Whether altering directions or changing our minds, when freed from preconceptions, we expand, expand, expand to the very limits of our potential!"

Teasingly, G's glance swept down the amplification of his own body, "Now I illustrate this capacity in my very form!" The two old friends giggled at his quip. "The ability to remain curious requires a surprising amount of courage, Agnes. You have this facility, and you should value it. It is much too easy to stay with what we already believe . . . on a trail we recognize. But we left the reliability of home for a path of discovery, did we not? We are thus en route to a place where wonder encounters doubt, and all things change."

The idea of all this transformation excited Agnes. Perhaps she too would grow and grow and grow!

G's rich voice startled Agnes back from her musings. "Neither this nor that, here nor there—I live now in the in-between, in the great open field of perpetual movement. This is the secret to my transformation! And comfort in this space of learning is what I discovered."

Considering their fall off the slide in the park, where G's stuffing had been literally knocked right out of him, Agnes understood just what G meant. With his head off, and everything inside it out, how he'd put himself back together was bound to be different! He'd been broken, but she realized that this was not a bad thing. Instead, it had initiated an opportunity, which G had seized. She looked up admiringly at the Golden Being standing larger than life in front of her. G had certainly made the most of what had been offered to him, and now he was a living demonstration of the very courage of which he spoke.

"You've been very brave, G. But I'm not sure I can do it," Agnes admitted. "I've been frightened on this journey— really, really scared—about a million times already!"

"Oh, but you can, Agnes . . . and you already have," he reassured her. "Courage simply necessitates the confidence to be yourself. To act as you know it is right to act—to act as *you*! To be heroic doesn't mean that you are not afraid. It means you act *despite* your fear . . . because you know the proper response."

G gestured toward the heavens. "Look to this vast sky, Agnes, to the moon and stars. Receive your bearings in their expansiveness. Each new threshold you cross is a choice, a chance to act in a certain way, to determine where you will place your commitment. Much like choosing which forest path to follow, we must allow change—even embrace it. Take a moment to be sure that what you are doing, what you are saying, is a choice. Your choice. Not a reaction, but truly your choice. Become certain that you are who you are.

That you act and speak as yourself. Then you are acting with integrity—and that is the gift that I found, Agnes. And of course," G added, winking broadly, "be careful not to lose your head!"

Again, both laughed delightedly at his jest. After what G had been through, who better understood the issues that arose with losing one's head?

So, they would continue to explore the forest, these good friends, continue to guide their way through this unknown territory, seeking the Lost Temple, keeping curiosity ever close at hand, their hearts and minds open to new passageways and new opportunities, meeting challenges together— with as much fortitude as a little Canadian girl and a formerly stuffed elephant could.

All the travelling companions gathered to welcome G back, peppering him with questions. It was a beautiful evening with a clear sky, and after listening to Agnes recount G's recommendation to look to its expansiveness for inspiration, the group reclined on the leaves of the forest to stare up into the night. The miracle of the Big Dipper's cosmic question mark mirrored the vastness of their own inner queries:

. . . *Just what is this mysterious Lost Temple and when will we finally find it?* (Agnes)

. . . *What path will best lead us to success in our quest?* (Streak)

. . . *What unimaginable perils are ahead and how will we conquer them?* (ChiChi)

. . . *What's for dinner?* (Finder)

73

In answer to all this wonder, G initiated a plan. The group watched in amazement as he spun about, his four arms becoming eight. Spinning again, eight swirled into sixteen, his hands bearing gifts—tools to aid his friends on their journey.

On the little girl, G bestowed a goad to gently prod her to stay the course, encouraging her to fulfill her dreams. For Streak, he had a lasso that captured the tiger's memories— an aggregate of all past tiger experiences. With this support, Streak's judgement would remain clear. For the cheetah, he extended an impressive treasure, one gifted to G on his own journey of transformation: a bow bent of sugarcane's sweet pliancy, a thousand honey bees humming its string. With it, five arrows tipped with delicately scented flowers ensured that ChiChi's aim would be true and his future seeded with fragrant promise.

Sometimes we all need a nudge, a bit of help in gathering our resources. Sometimes what's needed might seem like magic—a bit of ourselves propelled forward with only hope to forecast the yield. But with the right tools, and in the best company, we recognize that the magic is actually flowing from us and through us, and that hope is only a placeholder while we work toward our goals.

. . . Oh, and for the giraffe? Well, for him, G produced a sandwich. Being an exceptionally generous soul, Finder ensured that they each got to take a bite.

Big adventures make for big appetites.

8

remembrance

"I don't give up; I forget why not."

- DOROTHY PARKER

remembrance

Fog stretched its pale arm down the canyon. Only the narrowest of ledges held precariously to the mountainside. Veiled in cloud, the path virtually disappeared. Insecurity increased. To one side, the sheer cliff rose—a tremendous wall of rock and earth. On the other side, it plunged down just as sheerly. A long way down. Underfoot, small stones loosened and tumbled, rattling to the depths of the gorge and jangling the pilgrims' nerves. No one, it seemed, breathed.

The ashen clouds passed, then reappeared just as suddenly. The world was real, then simply a phantasm. And with each reappearance, the temperature dropped as precipitously as the ravine.

The group held close, each step cautious, bodies pressed to the cliffside. The sharp air cut through Agnes's thin dress, and she shivered. Such slow going. With his mile-long legs and skyscraper height, the giraffe was especially vulnerable. He picked his footing cautiously but still stumbled and faltered; his centre of gravity was much too high for this terrain.

Agnes worried, and again and again, called out, "Finder, are you okay? Are you okay?"

Adjusting his countenance to allay her concerns, the giraffe's confident smile failed to fully reassure. The little Canadian's brow puckered with intensity.

Finally, Streak—leading the group—stopped. "Might we pause awhile? A bit harum-scarum to continue, what? Perhaps the fog will clear a bit if we're patient," he suggested. With their refined balance, he knew that both he and ChiChi were fine, but the path's current condition caused him concern, and he was sensitive to the stresses affecting the others. Caution was most important, with a gradual advance preferable to complete disaster.

And so, they hesitated, each traveller clinging to the earthen wall. A hawk's screech haunted the distance, knitting them to the world beyond the clouds. Agnes's teeth began to chatter uncontrollably. Feeling a tug on her skirt, she was startled to look down and see a tiny man. Where had he come from?!

Recovering her manners, Agnes greeted him. "Hello! Who are you?" (Her chattering teeth made this sound more like *"Chello! Choo ahh choo?"*) A diminutive arm reached up and handed her a fuzzy shawl. She accepted gratefully, wrapping it tightly about her shoulders. Warming quickly, she tried again. "Thank you! That helps so much! What is your name?"

"Me? I am Apasssmara," the wee newcomer slurred quietly, his voice half-swallowed by the raging wind.

"I'm sorry!" Agnes bent low. "I couldn't quite hear you. Who are you?"

Apasmara was annoyed. He shouldn't be surprised, and yet, just once (just once!), he wished someone would recognize him. It was not to be. Indeed, how could it be otherwise?

"I am the Field of Forgetfulnesss!" Apasmara replied testily, his sibilants skidding. "And I am the Path to Remembranccce."

Poor Agnes frowned in bewilderment. Remembrance and Forgetfulness? "Can one be both?" she queried, with honest curiosity.

Apasmara returned her frown, seriously disgruntled. *Is this young girl not all there?* he wondered. *Why do all the celestials have their auras in a twist over this seemingly dim-witted child?*

Swivelling his small body, he looked directly up into her face, and in his barely audible voice, gave it one more try: "I am the circuitry; don't you sssee? I translate and adjust the processs. As one flows in, one flows out. One becomesss the other."

Agnes leaned in, hunkering down beside him. "I'm so very sorry! I can hardly hear you—it's the wind!" she explained, a bit embarrassed over her inability to decipher this tiny man's liquid hiss. "Would you please tell me your name once again?"

Somewhat assuaged by her civility, his susurrant voice repeated, "Apasssmara. I am here to help you."

"Why, that's really lovely!" She accepted his favour with joy, quite accustomed now to meeting strange beings along this journey. Agnes had encountered so much willingness to help her on her quest. *It really is a wonderful world,* she thought, *with oceans of kindnesses tendered so frequently.* She vowed that she too would swim in this ocean, always remembering to offer aid to anyone she could.

Softening at the sincerity of her warmth, the little man shook his head sadly. "Oh, but you will forget, Agnesss. Everyone always doesss!"

"Excuuuuse me?!" Agnes exaggerated, quite taken aback that her thoughts had been read. "What's in my mind is private, you know!" she chided.

"I'm sssorry!" came the slippery reply. *(Although it's still entirely true,* Apasmara assured himself.) "I know I shouldn't have said so, but you sssee, this is my very purview. That's what I'm trying to explain to you: everyone forgetsss. Although, of course, I don't like to be forgotten, forgetting itself is not a bad thing. Not at all!

"I exist as the continuity between Forgetfulnesss and Remembranccce. To accept one without the other suggests a state—when in truth, it's a process. You sssee? A flow of experience to recognition, recognition to reflection. Then the dismantling of it all until—once again, when remembering—you return to recognition.

"You think forgetting is simply—well, forgetting. Most everyone doesss!" Apasmara allowed. "Just as you believe this path you trek to be a single path, Agnesss. I have come to teach you that the way is never singular. Instead, it is paved with diverse options. In that manner too, forgetfulness and remembranccce share. What you choose to forget, what you choose to remember. Perhaps I can offer a suggestion or two to aid you in your navigation?"

Under the tight wrap of her shawl, Agnes shrugged woolly shoulders, the tilt of her chin clearly indicating that she remained unconvinced.

"Do you not believe there is value to forgetting, little girl?" he inquired, quite miffed. Apasmara's body remained low to the ground, but his tone began to rise haughtily. So that this willful child might better comprehend, he whispered with all his might: "Life carries us through many emotionsss. But each must relinquish its position to allow another to take its placcce. Heartache, I give—yet through me, heartache dissipates as well. As it must. Do you sssee? Fears quiet, anger easesss. How could one carry on, if one remained captive to their suffocation?"

Nodding to her tiny new friend, Agnes agreed. "Yes, yes. I do see what you're saying—of course, you're quite right! You help lessen pain, don't you? When we forget? That's definitely a good thing!" Agnes considered how, just last night, she'd tossed about restlessly in the anguish of missing her sister and brother. Only when her thoughts had moved elsewhere could she finally sleep.

But at this humiliating simplification of the adroitness of his skill, Apasmara's face contorted in disgust. "It's not simply bad things you forget!" he countered as sharply as his soft voice would allow. Really, he was so often underestimated, and well . . . let's face it . . . no one enjoyed that. Frankly, it hurt!

"All emotions must move. This is life itself. Fear, anger, heartache—of course." Apasmara was clearly provoked. "But delight diminishes as well, does it not? And only then can we return to revel in its pleasures once again. Anticipation, surprise, serenity, joy—it mattersss not. All must ease. All must be depleted so that they might return again. Can you not sssee that it is only if the depth of wonder is forgotten that we can experience itsss renewal?" He had Agnes there, and she conceded graciously. Though diminutive in stature, the breadth of his arguments could not be minimized.

"We put aside what we have learned to allow what more we might learn," the tiny man lisped quietly. "We cannot grow without making space for doubt, without listening for opportunities, without the curiosity to attempt the novel. We create ourselves—then re-create ourselves—through our inquiriesss. In this manner, we grow, we build, we expand . . . and we rediscover. It is from me, you sssee, that each day dawns anew. That each season emerges fresssh. It is from me that imagination's deep well springs ever forth. Ask yourself what, indeed, would remain precious, if we did not recognize the fragility of its existenccce, that change itself is inevitable, and that all things passs?"

His pride not yet ready to be silenced, Apasmara continued, struggling to clearly convey his message. "It is I, after all, who ensures that we never truly forget where we came from. I remain. I remain. Ever underfoot. I am petite—you might have noticed." (Indeed, she had!) "Constantly, you'll find me entangled as we unexpectedly trip over our recollectionsss. We are built of the experience of memories, yet unconsciousness too is always present within that narrative—it touches everything, you sssee? We are the embodiment of all our experiences—whether painful or pleasurable, whether remembered *or* forgotten. Still, I remain. I remain. I am in the way you hold yourself, the manner in which you walk and move. I am etched into your body from everything you have ever done. I live in your skin, in your muscles and sinew and blood. Ever-present. Yet not easily found. You might only glimpse me—as formless as a fog.

"You might hear me, but only as a murmur." Agnes bent close as Apasmara stated the obvious, his whisper riding a gust to her ears. "And so, my very voice acts as memory. Don't you sssee? You must pay attention! Listen closely to your recollections, otherwise they are lost on the wind. As scent too, I can haunt you. Lingering. Or startle you as a familiar movement. I live as hints, as insinuations, as murmured suggestionsss. This is my way."

The pattern of his arguments swirled about her like the clouds in the canyon until comprehension cleared her mind, and Agnes nodded.

She considered the varying tasks and hobbies that created the people she knew. Mrs. Mary Eleven, hobbling through her garden, her back irreparably bent after eighty years of duress. Momma, her hands as gnarled as a beautiful tree by her willing engagement in hard work. The airy step of the ballerina next door, who never seemed to touch the ground. That boy down the street—his body hard with muscle—obsessively lifting weights in the backyard. Experience created all of this physical diversity! Yet what Apasmara was sharing led Agnes to grant that habits of thought, and patterns of belief, also contribute to shape.

"Yesss! All the choices you have made, all these you hold in your form!" Ignoring the disapproval Agnes shot his way once again, Apasmara disconcertingly responded to her thoughts.

"Your body is a story told, young one. A treasure box of the passst. Experiences, whether forgotten or remembered, are the stuff upon which your very bones change, the stuff of which your memories are constructed. But your tendons and muscles also are built of them. And of course, not just your own experiencesss!"

His voice heavy with rebuke, again he cautioned against over-simplification. "You reflect the history of your people, little girl—the history of all humanity. For you grow as in soil: the soil of culture, of clan, of your moment in time. Do you sssee? Do you sssee?" His voice raised as passion flamed his argument.

"I do," she whispered back into the wind, eyes rapt. This was proving to be a wild ride, and Agnes was intent on understanding the little man's very big story.

"From me, what is past wanes to background, creating room for attention elsewhere. I curve, always curve, looking back. I twist to witness what has come before." His thin voice lowered in a chortle. "Don't worry; your memories are safe with me."

Lifting his abbreviated blade, its tip shiny and very sharp, Apasmara added, "My knife combats fear, as fear often accompanies what is new. There must be risk in order to learn. But fear is a fire too easily stoked. I carry this knife as a reminder that you have tools at your disposal. You are never bereft. I keep my sword ever ready to trim what might be trimmed—what must be trimmed. And from my pieces, you reassemble, returning them to consciousnessss. In this way, you 're-member.'

"All things end, young one. But when we foresee that completion, too much urgency followsss. So, I obscure endings, hide them from you, so that the experience itself may be without restraint. Sorrow or joy unlimited, you sssee? Forget. Remember. New and now."

His low tones slipped through Agnes, a slippery voice snaking inside, difficult to catch—to hold. Barely audible, just a humming hint of sound that she winnowed out of the howling air.

"Like a dream?" he asked, reading her expression.

Ignoring his continued access to her thoughts, she agreed. "Yes." Her dreams did haunt her like vapours, and she realized that often her recollections did as well. Not quite firm, they remained secluded in her heart, in her mind, and in her body, needing to be coaxed from their hiding place like shy animals—just like Apasmara's murmuration. Everything around her dropped away as she focused on his fragile voice.

Unwillingly, consternation rumpled her forehead. Apasmara reached out. Tiny hand met tiny hand. Patiently now, he continued. "It is through that pulse of memories obscured, then coalesced back into view, that you discover the fullness of yourself. Forgetfulness, remembrance—both are giftsss! Like my knife, you might call them tools, if you wisssh. Which tool will you choose to hold, my dear? And what will be so undervalued that it remains unrecognized? What will be so painful that it necessitates diminishment? What mundane recurrence will you cherish again and again, writing that thought or action into your very form? What ache will be so undeniable, so debilitating, that it must be hidden so that you might carry on? These are your human riches, are they not, young one? These riches are what instigate sentimentsss. Do you know that even the Shining Ones themselves admire this human attribute? This ability to feel? Emotions create the secret opening, you sssee. They create the portal to growth.

"Listen, my dear," Apasmara whispered, sinking his own vision deep into the little Canadian girl's eyes. Agnes gripped his every word. "Here is the opportunity to achieve humanity's most stunning phenomenon: the ability to pass like a miracle into the skin of another. To relate, to share—even to exchange—with other beings. It is born of this very facility, is it not? For it is within this reciprocity that you might live the experience of another."

Agnes's eyebrows lifted. This tiny man was revealing something immense. And immensely kind. Within the inseparable relationship of forgetting and remembering, as emotions morph continuously like scudding clouds, the seeds of empathy root, then sprout. What a gift, indeed!

Recognizing the success of his undertaking, Apasmara challenged the little girl. "So, when you sense me underfoot, Agnesss, dance ever lightly! Allow me the freedom to quell your fearsss. Allow me the freedom to ferry your memories, to alleviate your distresss. Keep me close. Keep me close, and empathy will indeed grow within you. You will see through another's eyesss. You will feel as they feel. Whether in anguish or elation, expand yourself in empathy, and you will nurture true wisdom."

The fog crept forward again, blanching distinctions.

"Don't forget me!" sighed the soft voice, plaiting itself into the wind. "Yet, of course, you will . . . as it must be. I curve. I curve. From me, each moment shapes itself in rebirth."

Agnes could no longer hear him, though, as both his voice and form had faded back into the clouds.

9
love

"The only way to make sense out of change
is to plunge into it, move with it, and join the dance."

- ALAN WATTS

love

Its source cloaked in deep shadow, a sinuous melody twined through the forest.

"Mmmmm . . . I hearrrrr music!" Streak purred, quivering his sleek stripes. ChiChi's sharp ears caught it too, and entangled in its enchanting melody, spotted fur pulsed. Soon all the companions swayed to the tender tune, eyes hooded in soft rapture.

It was the dark night of the moon, a time of introspection. The travellers had been silent all day, lost in the corridors of their thoughts, when this musical seduction began. Its cadence seemed familiar yet the inflection utterly new. All moved then to a song that was singular, celebrating this delight within their own hearts.

When it stopped, the group awoke as if from a dream. Drowsily, they looked to one another as light laughter glimmered around them, tumbling over the scales like a jazzman, the player still unseen. An ambiance of joy pervaded, and the pilgrims waited, unhurried, arrested in this suspended moment of overwhelming pleasure.

Recognizing the unmistakable atmosphere, G shouted out, "Krishna—join us!", causing Agnes to cast a glance of suspicion his way.

Into the clearing sauntered an iridescent boy, his youthful charismatic glory shimmering a peacock's sheen. A Rock Star, he trailed an entourage in his wake, and soon the forest was full of chatter and hubbub, of bewitching girls in fancy clothes, of festive cows and frolicking goats. Of coloured ornaments and hanging lanterns, flounces, frills, and glittering spangles. Of sensual perfumes and the rich odour of delicious food. The companions licked their lips in anticipation.

G threw his arms about the boy in hearty welcome, kissing him fondly on both cheeks, then again. Krishna greeted them all, charming each individually with his wit, his warmth, his irresistible joie-de-vivre.

With no further ado, his eyes full of mischief and glee, the boy pulled out his flute. "Shall we dance?" And without waiting for a reply, Krishna wove a rollicking tune that had them dancing until their feet were sore, until their clothes were drenched in salty sweat, until exhaustion waved over them and the munchies raged.

"PICNIC!" the giraffe yelled, and the party girls spread their silken shawls. The group ate and chatted and joked and ate some more. They told humorous stories and posed the Big Questions. Shared their dreams. Then—deeply in love with one another and the lavish abundance of their full hearts—they laid their heads back and enjoyed the dance moves of the stars in the moonless sky.

Rosy dawn finally warmed the horizon. The girls yawned and packed up their wraps. Agnes laid her hand on Krishna's beautiful dark arm and thanked him for this convivial night.

"I came to offer my music to those who seek the Lost Temple," Krishna replied. "My song is the song inside each one of us, the song that longs to be sung. In the sky of this Dark Moon, we savoured the discovery of boundless stars. Know also that you have your own infinite worlds within the darkness you carry inside."

"I don't see them," Agnes answered, unsure.

"Like the twinkling light of the stars, real beauty is found deep within the darkness. It is not your eyes that will show you. It is your heart that will lead." He winked. "If you allow it—as you reflect upon the shadows within—the light will find you. Then, like the images we concoct and call constellations, new connections can be made. You create your own constellations to inform the magic of your inner sky."

Agnes felt the glow of this gorgeous night, but she was also full of the allure the others had experienced. *Is this what love does to us?* she wondered, for it was truly impossible not to fall in love with this Brilliant Being. "Oh, I wish you could stay and travel with us, Krishna!"

His laughter was sweet. "Why, I am always with you, dear one. In the prism on a raindrop, you will find me. In the satisfaction of a game well-played. In the torrent of a waterfall, the precious song of the morning's first robin. I am in that ditty that G whistles incessantly, in Streak's liquid purr. When you lift ChiChi's spirits with a tickle, or scratch that special place between Finder's brows. In love's light, I am always with you! I am here in every joy you manifest from inside. In every passion. In every moment you truly love your life."

"I will miss your song," the little Canadian girl insisted.

"That can never happen, my sweet!" His joy beamed back to her, reassuringly. "For you are the song the universe is singing." And as he melted into the forest shadows, he called back, "I am here. I am here. I am always here . . ."

waxing crescent

IO

water

"In fact, your heart is made to break;
its purpose is to burst open again and again,
so it can hold ever more wonders."

- ANDREW HARVEY

water

The tropical heat had become intense. The pilgrims began to travel after sunset, cooled, secreted by shadows. Though the moon now waxed to a delicate curve, they remained dependent on the night vision of Streak and ChiChi and the eerie glow of the luminous giraffe.

Fears grow with sudden urgency under evening's dusky veil, and when two ember-like eyes crept toward the group, hearts sped and breath quickened. Guarding the group behind them, the two cats ruffled up, stoically waiting for the mysterious being behind rubicund eyes to make the first move.

A voice of gravel and sand addressed them: "Greetings from the Goddess! She Who Shifts Continents! She Who Spins Tales! She Who Rides the River's Whims! She Who Breaks

Only to Break, Then Breaks Again! It is she who welcomes you to her River."

Mightily impressed by this striking formality, eyes shifted sidelong as the companions wondered what to do next.

From the shadows a massive crocodile slithered forward; as one, the group took a rapid step back. Sinuously, the armoured beast advanced again. The travellers retreated. Forward, back. Forward, back.

"Please STOP!" the exasperated crocodile admonished. "The Goddess has sent me to guide you. Her River will be your most treacherous challenge yet, and you will need her help to understand the essence of the Waters. I will lead you to the other shore."

G motioned them all to gather closer to the imposing ruby-eyed reptile.

"You fear." The crocodile was plain-spoken.

"Hmmmph! A load of utter tosh," the tiger muttered. The cheetah joined Streak, grumbling his own disapproval of this statement. Affirming the obvious, though, Finder simply shrugged his shoulders and grimaced. G and Agnes cocked their heads, certain there was more to come.

Indeed, there was.

"Your fear stems from life's insecurities," the crocodile gargled. "Your friends, your neighbourhood—you wish for them to remain the same, to be what you have come to know. It is to introduce the way of the Goddess that she has sent me. For to discover the Lost Temple, you must learn to surrender to uncertainty.

"Climb upon me!" he issued an abrasive invitation. "Together we will enter her Waters. There, you will understand. Mirth will wash you, then Compassion. The next wave might bring Utter Disgust—perhaps Black Fury. Then Wonder of Wonders. Perhaps even Terror will find you, as is occasionally the case. Great Sadness too, of course, as Love sometimes leaves us with only its memory."

The faces of the poor companions filled with dread—this was all sounding rather dire.

"You will be unable to steel yourself against expectation," the crocodile cautioned, red eyes gleaming. "Just as in her Waters, there can be no preparation. Yes, the Horrifying dwells here, as it does in all worlds. But also, my friends, you will find Joy . . . Awe . . . and above all, Trust."

Inhaling a great collective breath, the friends readied themselves. Claws, hooves, G's many hands, and little Canadian fingers gripped the vast expanse of the reptile's craggy back.

"Remember: fight her River, and you will become distraught, grief-laden, exhausted from your unnecessary labour." In response to his warning, fingers, claws, toes, and hooves dug harder into gnarled skin, as the crocodile slithered toward the riverbank.

"Sir," Agnes gently cajoled. "Won't you please offer us guidance?"

He nodded. "Watch the moonlight on her Waters. Enter the fracturing shapes. Enter the sparkling. Employ their dizzying beauty as your own. Give yourself fully and surrender to the current. Then—only then—will you flow with her and acknowledge the gifts that come." With these last gritty words of advice, the massive hulk dove straight into the roiling darkness of the waves.

The crew clung desperately to his back.

SWIRLING!

TWIRLING!

WHIRLING!

Revolving like the very Earth itself, the crocodile spun on his own powerful axis.

Swollen surges of feeling!

Spiralling multicoloured emotions!

Fractal rainbows of sensation!

The valiant companions clenched the reptile's writhing musculature as he churned jagged shards of light and electricity, fluid waves, and streaming swells. All the transformative moments that break our hearts and change things forever wheeled over the travellers, passing through them like flashes of a remembered melody.

Some waves felt as granular as the crocodile's voice. Others oozed by, smoothly unctuous. There were smells too—rank, as well as luscious. Every sensation brought memories. More and more memories.

Through it all, the pilgrims held fast. Until, like a miracle, ongoing dizziness broke their resolve, and they found themselves no longer holding on but instead a very part of the great crocodile's strength, as liquid as the surges and swells of the flowing water.

Was it calmer now? Who's to say? Buoyant and free, they moved without effort.

SWIRLING!

TWIRLING!

WHIRLING!

With a final splash, a final tingle, a final wash of mood— with the taste of Love's Lasting on their lips—as promised, the crocodile deposited the companions on the river's far shore. Gratitude saturated them, and they thanked him for his help.

Desire trumping propriety, Agnes probed, "Can we not meet the Goddess?"

His sandy voice bemused, the crocodile answered simply. "You have been with her. You have been with her all along." Ruby eyes began to sink slowly beneath the waves as he gargled back to them, "She is here. She is here. Now. And always. In the water . . . in the water . . ."

Swiftly lifting their eyes, the friends witnessed shards of light crackling across the river. Flashing, multicoloured prisms danced an erratic sequence, then fractured like lightning on the water's surface. Ripples rose and fell in perfect imperfection . . . or was it imperfect perfection?

For indeed it was she: She Who Breaks Only to Break, Then Breaks Again.

II
fire

"'Would you tell me, please,
which way I ought to go from here?'
'That depends a good deal on where you want to get to.'"

- LEWIS CARROLL

fire

Drying off their memories, the small band of seekers remained huddled at the river's edge, tender still from the deluge of their swirling emotions. This kaleidoscope of feelings had left them all rather disoriented.

In recovery, Streak and ChiChi groomed one another with purpose; being cats, this could take some time. Stripes and spots alike required attention.

"My blood sugar's dropping like a ripe mango," Finder whined. "Hmmm . . . a ripe mango . . ." Lanky tongue sloshed over thick lips, and off he ambled to find snacks.

The little Canadian girl's mind continued to gyrate. She felt sure she had recognized the sign the goddess had shimmered across the waves. Lines, triangles, circles . . . Its seeming randomness masked an elaborate pattern that reminded her of . . . of what? A broad shadow fell across her, disrupting her deliberations. Focusing, she saw G standing expectantly in front of her. She looked up, past his capacious belly, and met his kind gaze.

"Cold?" G asked.

She hadn't noticed, but soaked to her skin, she realized that G was right. "Freeeeezing," she chattered. He widened his four arms, and Agnes cuddled in close. He knew she was tired. Maybe a little grumpy too. Perhaps now was the right moment to fess up to the heavy secret he'd been harbouring. It might be tricky. Yes, definitely tricky, requiring tact. A gentle touch. Wisely, G began by travelling a circumspect route.

"We may have temporarily lost the path, my dear Agnes, but our intention need not desert us!" Agnes tipped her head quizzically.

"Reaching the Lost Temple is your intention—our intention," G quickly corrected himself. "But is it irrepressible? An irrepressible obsession?"

"Whaddya mean, G?" He frowned at her sloppy elocution but let it go. Now was not the time, as something more substantial was at stake.

"Well, Agnes," he continued, "every challenging task carries the potency to yield a remarkable revelation—one beyond your wildest expectations. But even realizing a dream takes focus and effort! Beginning might seem easy enough, when excitement and anticipation carry us on their great wave. Time and struggle, though, might still that wave. Our dedication dissipates, and we might consider giving up, sure that the goal is unreachable. Too difficult. It is only by embracing the unexpected that the really big magic can reach its promise."

He can be terribly pedantic sometimes, Agnes considered. *But holy smoke! What G doesn't know isn't worth knowing!*

"What you expect might never ever happen. But the unexpected? That, my dear," G assured her, "that will most certainly occur—one of the lessons of the River Goddess, no?" She nodded, so G continued.

"You must hold that, Agnes. Be receptive to it. Occasionally, the unexpected may arouse disappointment. Dormant sensations of doubt and timidity may also awaken, and we must utilize our deepest inner fortitude to counter them. Sometimes, though, it is those very unpredictable events that will astonish us with their fortuitousness. Serendipity can be most playful!" he added warmly. "The result is that commitment counts, as does persistence. You must be there when chance turns to face you. Commitment and persistence. It is your intention that knits these together."

Like a conductor's baton, G's trunk lifted and fell as he became more pledged to his argument. "To choose the pathway of discovery will ask everything of you," his wagging trunk emphasized. "In order to stay your course, obsession remains the wisest choice. Surrender to your own ardour. This is the fertile field in which you will locate the fire in your belly, the joy in your heart. It is in this open field, Agnes, this field of passion, where your effort—planted like a seed—will experience the miracle of growth."

With a furrowed brow, Agnes squinted up at him, G's newly magnificent girth shielding her view of much else. "If anyone can teach me the way to expand," she giggled mischievously, "it'd be you, G."

Groaning a bit at her gentle teasing, G was not swayed from his didactic trajectory. "What challenge asks of you, Agnes, is artistry!"

"Artistry?! But G, you know I'm no artist."

At this, G could not hold himself back. "I am not an artist," he corrected. "Really, Agnes—you do know better."

Holding tight to her disgruntled mood, the little girl only shrugged.

Determined to shift her from her funk, G carried on. "No artist, you claim. Really? Are you not, Agnes? If we place enough value upon it, if we care to do things right, we make art of everything we do. Be mindful, I'm not speaking of the artefact produced, but of the process of creation itself. Art is an action. A verb. It is transformation and communication. And art is also an attitude, an impassioned devotion to the details. Through the currency of your attention, you tell the world—tell yourself—just what you believe is vital.

"It's like justice," G offered as an example. "Justice would simply be a concept, just an idea, if we as a culture didn't decide it was to be cherished, to be honoured, even fought for. You see, Agnes, we all maintain the ability to decide where to place a boundary. We say this and not that. Now and not then. In placing that boundary, we declare it sacred ground. We decide what will not stand—and choose exactly what it is we will stand for."

Streak and ChiChi purred their approval. The cats were well-acquainted with living life as art, each action precise, each moment enjoyed—whether a moment of the simplest pleasure or one that demanded a dive into the deepest of personal reserves. As fully committed to relaxation as they were to the hunt, in their world, they were all in. All the time.

"Your art is the secret that will guide you through darkness like a beacon." Tenderly, G smiled down at her. "Creativity is that beacon, Agnes; it is the very light itself. To grow, to change, your creativity must remain ever present. And what is creativity? Imagination, certainly," G suggested. "A willingness to be receptive to a new plan or a fresh opportunity."

"Hope!" the cheetah opined.

"Yes, ChiChi!" G agreed. "You're right. Hope opens us to the states of possibility."

Streak joined in. "Resourcefulness, what?"

"Indeed!" G nodded. "We can't leave ourselves wanting! We must be exigent, using what is at hand. Agnes, you hold all these powers, my dear. You hold them within yourself, as each of us does. They are life's gift. You have what you need. And to activate those resources, to utilize them, is simplicity itself. Simply offer your gratitude for the gift. That is all. Love your life, Agnes. Love every minute of it!"

Agnes appreciated her friends' attempts to smooth her dented spirits—she really did. Yet all their efforts still couldn't ease her disappointment at her inability to decipher the message the goddess had offered. That ephemeral sparkle had held meaning, of that she was certain. Yet it eluded her, dissolving like a mirage. Not being able to understand it really had her self-annoyance at full measure.

G refused to give up. "I know a lot about this from my own transformational process, Agnes. Not only can I now do things that I couldn't before, but what I've experienced is also what we've all been through here! Change instigates a different way of thinking. While I might have grown in more obvious ways," G motioned to his new body, "you are growing too. Everything we do, every idea we have, every plan we make . . . these all affect us. Change us. And we grow. We grow constantly. Don't allow discouragement to undermine your confidence. Stay committed to your intention." Within her despondency, Agnes heard Apasmara's teachings echoed in G's words. Still . . .

G circled back to his original point. "Allow yourself to be held in this eternal moment of becoming, Agnes. In this growing. In fact . . ." G hesitated before cracking open a bit more of his secret. *Desperate times, needs must, and all that.* "An idea has occurred, my dear. Actually, I'd be more correct to state that several ideas have occurred." With humour as well as humility—so attractive in such a Great Being—he winked broadly, then, without warning, abruptly stood. Sent off-kilter, Agnes pitched to the forest floor.

"What gives?!" Her tone still peevish, she dusted leaves from her frock, a bit of mud from her cheek.

"You're going to need to get ready for this, Agnes."

Like fractal origami, the Girthful One then unfurled his single elephant head into five. Ten eyes now gazed down at her, instead of two. Five trunks curled this way and that. "I will look simultaneously in all directions and gather the necessary information to make our next decision," he explained.

A shock, no doubt. "HOLY SMOKE, G! What the . . .?! First four arms; now five heads!" Agnes—who by rights should have grown accustomed to the miraculous occurring—was still wowed. Not quite ready to give way, though, she indulged in more self-pity, shaking her sole head in lone frustration. She dramatically prolonged a fat sigh. "How lucky you are to have five heads to rely upon, dear G!"

Tilting his chin, chin, chin (you get the idea!), he gazed down at her and laughed. Enough of this mollycoddling!

"AGNES!"

Startled by G's sharpened voice, both spotted and striped fur stood on end. Agnes found her full height.

"Draw on your own five as well!" G commanded. Uncomprehending, Agnes frowned, her obtuseness eliciting more mirth.

"AGNES!" She straightened another millimetre in response to his booming voice. "Disappointment is dulling your senses. What is it you smell? What is it you hear?"

In a flash of insight, her single head nodded in recognition. Of course, of course. Her five senses! And with this bit of magic—the magic of a fresh perspective, the magic of hope and resourcefulness—her stubborn gloomy spell

113

was broken. One idea soon became five. Five ideas became ten. The friends chattered excitedly, as the firestorms of their imaginations conjured cleverness out of the humid jungle air. All they needed now was a bit of sustenance.

And at that moment—at just precisely the right moment—Finder gambolled up, chanting, "Mangos! Mangos! Mangos!" Agnes smiled. She loved mangos! But then, who didn't?

With that, G lifted his left leg and began to whirl to his right, spinning a fierce vortex of a dance. Alongside this Great Being—so light of heart, so light of step—the little Canadian girl danced too. The tiger danced. The cheetah danced. And on his tremulous, stilty legs, the giraffe danced as well. Deep into the night, the party of friends partied, laughter providing all the rhythm they needed, their earlier chill long forgotten within the warmth of shared joy.

Grace. Always there when we least expect it.

12

wind

"All things depend on each other.
Everything breathes together."

- PLOTINUS

wind

Abandoning G and the giraffe to their tiffin, the two cats to their nap, Agnes ventured a short walkabout of her own. Discovering an aerie with an expansive vista of the Lost Temple in the far distance, she perched on its high ledge and looked out.

The Temple's four tremendous gateways pierced the green canopy, each ornamenting a cardinal direction. *Will we enter through those?* Agnes mused. Creeper vines wound round and round the temple columns, teaching their protracted lessons in patience, their curving growth seeping eventual fissures into the granite facade. A central citadel lifted its rooftop finials to glimmer under the sun. *Are these golden peaks our goal?*

The Temple remained a great way off. Agnes heaved a sigh as high as its soaring gates, as thick as its stone ramparts.

A sigh as complex as each ornately carved pillar. They had trekked for days and days and days now, and while G's talk had buoyed her, again she found herself somewhat dejected to witness the incredible distance yet to be covered. *Why these low spirits?* she wondered. The journey so far had been miraculous—full of adventures, discoveries, and friendship. Perhaps she was simply a bit sleepy . . .

A rustle from behind interrupted her ruminations, and she looked up, expecting her companions. Instead, there emerged from the forest a tall monkey. A very, very tall monkey. A monkey with a most distinguished presence, a bit of a beard, and large inky eyes. Without a word, he settled his slim figure beside her, his black eyes fixed on the far horizon.

"Hello," she initiated tentatively.

"Hello," he repeated back without even a glance her way. *Hmmmm,* she thought, *so not your usual chattering monkey.*

Another attempt: "Do you live around here?"

"No," his laconic response.

Okaaaay . . .

Accepting his reserve, Agnes turned back to the scene before her. And so, they perched together on the ridge, the girl and the monkey, staring out quietly across the roof of the forest to the great temple complex beyond. A few buzzards looped their black cauldron in the sky. Lazy in the heat, a fat fly buzzzzed. And since sitting in silence was so rarely practiced—except amongst the most comfortable of friends—the girl soon felt her heart opening to this breviloquent simian.

"You are afraid," the monkey stated finally. "That is why your spirits fail you. But courage without consideration will not prevail."

A gentle encouragement.

"You are near. Nearer than you think. Yet what you do next requires a great leap. I myself have made many. Some call them 'leaps of faith,' but I prefer to think of them as Leaps of Confidence. For it is only when my self-confidence surges that I feel truly ready."

Agnes sought his further tutelage. "How did you find that confidence, sir?"

"Its foundation is established in my relationship with friends. I see their belief in me mirrored in their eyes. Lift off requires this firm foundation. Its support is paramount. Do you have friends?" he pressed. "Good friends?"

"Oh yes!" she replied without hesitation. "The best."

"Does their love reflect back to you? It is an echo, is it not? It comes back only as it goes out."

Agnes nodded her agreement—no doubt about it!

The monkey continued. "My father is Wind. When I leap, I call upon him."

Agnes sighed emphatically, shaking her head. This would be more problematic. "That's very magical, but my father is definitely not the wind."

"Will you close your eyes and listen?" the monkey asked.

She did as the monkey asked. Her eyes closed, and she simply listened—listened to the wind.

The breeze, as languorous as her new friend's language, blew its gentle sibilance through the leaves. It was indistinguishable from the sound of her breath, and her unrest seeped into the ground with each exhalation, her buoyancy increasing with a fresh intake of breath.

"I breathe out, and you breathe in," the monkey explained. "A small wind, you might think. Too ordinary for you to notice. Yet, a wind. You exhale. My inhalation rushes in. Is this not magic? Each breath ignites the sparkle of life. A small wind. The tiniest wind. Yet in its transparent tenderness, it carries the power of all existence. If asked what a breath looks like, we might respond, what does life look like? So, you are quite correct. It is magic!"

Opening her eyes, Agnes found she couldn't argue. "Well, I hadn't thought about it just that way," she admitted. "You've got a point. It is pretty miraculous!"

The monkey carried on. "Like snowflakes, no two breaths are exactly alike. Can you note the difference between each? Listen carefully to develop this skill."

Again, the little girl closed her eyes. Together, they listened. Agnes could hear the monkey inhaling and exhaling and effortlessly matched his rhythm. In each breath received, in each breath released, she soon found that a distinct intonation presented itself. An exclamation of wonder escaped her lips, and optimism began to twinkle in Agnes's bright smile.

"And is this too not extraordinary?" the monkey teased a bit cheekily, encouraged at the success of his arguments. "Allow yourself the full fascination of the magic," he counselled.

Agnes felt her breath travelling slowly through her body, felt its sinuous path, felt its seductive pleasures. Indeed, as her new friend suggested, each breath expressed its own texture, its intrinsic qualities affecting her mood.

"So," the monkey concluded, "do we not all share the gift of Wind's sustenance? Do we not all experience this presence?" Cheerily, Agnes nodded her agreement.

The monkey was not yet done. "It is said that I alter my size at will. This is true." Standing, he was even taller—much taller—than she recalled. "You too have this power!"

The little Canadian girl prepared herself to become big—much bigger than her sister! She bent her head to her chest, eyes squeezed tightly, body tense. *This is going to be sooooo great!* (Adding to her height was a favourite fantasy.)

The monkey laughed at the sight of her, then shook his head. "No, no! It is more obvious than that! We speak of Wind. Notice well: each breath expands you!"

Relaxing, Agnes inhaled deeply. And indeed, she felt her ribs expand, her back and her chest widen, her belly grow. "Exhaling, you get smaller once again," noted the monkey. And of course, she did.

"Do you see now, young one?" the monkey inquired kindly. "The magical is not only all around you—it lives within you. Take nothing for granted. You will soon realize that we are surrounded by small miracles every day. Everything about life is incredible."

The monkey opened his palm to Agnes. "Look!"

In a hushed voice, she acknowledged the perfection of the delicate blossom nestled there. "It's so beautiful!"

The monkey nodded. "Yes. Now look again!" he directed, stretching his hand closer to Agnes.

"Ooooooh!" Agnes murmured, only then spying that, within its rosy petals, a chubby bee slept, dreaming a pink dream. "Cuuuuute!" she whispered, so as not to wake it.

"Miracles within miracles. Magic within magic. Many would diminish the magic, dismiss it as the quotidian. Yet life is truly a series of wonders," he said. "Of embedded treasures. You are curious, little one. Of course, that is why you are here, in this forest. So, I believe you already know this, but . . . keep your wonder ever with you! It is a valuable gift, yet fragile. Nourish it. Attend to it. If ignored, you may find you have lost it. If ignored, it simply disappears."

"Really?" She was startled that something that seemed without end could evaporate.

"Oh, yes. It's quite common. Along the way, people may forget to remain aware. They fall into habits. Once they have seen something, they believe they understand it. Curiosity withers quickly once certainty arrives! Without attention, well . . . wonder dies." Sadness shivered through him from his heart to his head. "As you grow, Agnes, let your curiosity grow too. Bring it with you wherever you go. It will always lead you to discovery."

Agnes pressed for specifics. "How do I do that, sir?"

"Call to it as you grow and change," he suggested. "Shout to it, when you are moving, 'Come along! Come along!' Invite it to remain always by your side, as you would a valued friend. Recognize that it *lives*, for it is within curiosity that your spirit resides—the full expression of your being. Attend to it, and it will remain one of your powers."

"ONE of my powers?" Agnes squeaked a little in her excitement.

"Of course!" the monkey responded adamantly. "We all have myriad powers. Phenomenal powers! Both shared gifts and those that remain quite distinctly your own. Engage them and claim them, young one! It's very easy."

Generously, he offered to demonstrate. "Will you try with me?"

Her trust complete, Agnes smiled. "Definitely!"

wind's meditation
a practice

"No meaning but what we find here.
No purpose but what we make."

- GREGORY ORR

"Close your eyes," the monkey began. "Feel the ground beneath you. Now stretch tall from your heavy seat. Keep your eyes soft. Relax your jaw.

"Envision a small bubble in your mind's eye. It floats in front of you, as easeful as you yourself remain.

"As you inhale, see the bubble grow. As you exhale, it diminishes.

"You inhale; the bubble expands. It hovers for a moment in the space of your mind. You exhale; it shrinks in size once again.

"Inhale . . . enlarge the bubble. On your long exhalation, the bubble follows your lead, minimizing as that breath leaves you.

"Inhale. Exhale. The bubble expands . . . The bubble contracts . . .

"Inhale. Exhale. The bubble expands . . . The bubble contracts . . .

"As it enlarges, the skin of the bubble grows so thin you can see right through it. In your mind's eye, it sheens with multiple colours as the sun warms its surface.

"Inhale. Exhale. The bubble expands . . . The bubble contracts . . .

"Inhale. Exhale. The bubble expands . . . The bubble contracts . . .

"Now bring that bubble inside. Encourage it to enter your body, to float inside you. Feel it expand on your in-breath, and gently subside on your out-breath. Inhale, it grows. Exhale, and the surface of the bubble gets tighter, the bubble ebbs.

"Feel your own skin to be as thin as that of the bubble. It feels the sun. It feels the movement. Breathe in . . . Breathe out. Breathe in . . . Breathe out.

"Your body widens, then gets smaller again. Remain pliant. Permeable. Your own body as malleable as the bubble. Breathe in . . . Breathe out . . .

"Easy inhalations. Restful exhalations.

"Like a sphere, you feel the movement in all directions as you breathe.

"Release any sense of effort. Allow air to move through you as smoothly as possible. Not too full, not too empty. Easy. Just easy . . . Breathe in . . . Breathe out . . ."

After five minutes, Agnes heard the monkey's confident voice once again. "Now simply sit quietly. Breathe naturally," he advised. "Enjoy the sensations in your body."

The little girl felt the contentment that surrounded her as palpably as the breeze on her skin. Life was indeed a wonder! Gently, her eyes opened and adjusted to the light.

Brushing twigs from her frock, Agnes stood to meet the monkey's tranquil gaze.

Layering his hands over his heart, eyes dark and fathomless, he invited her in. Without pause, without question, she leapt—into his eyes . . . and into his heart. And at the very same moment, she found that he had jumped into hers.

"I am Hanuman," he said, then turned and vanished into the trees.

13

creativity

"For my part, I know nothing with any certainty,
but the sight of the stars makes me dream."

- VINCENT VAN GOGH

creativity

Streak sang out in excitement. "What ho! What ho! What ho!" Elation rang into the forest, for the travellers had finally arrived at one of the immense temple gates. While overgrown with tangled creepers, this outer portal into the temple grounds marked a way in. Everyone was jubilant.

Agnes looked to G, who lifted one eyebrow quizzically. What to do next? While passing through the opulent entry seemed obvious, confronted with a destination that had seemed so far off for so long—had been desired so intently, and moved toward so diligently—wouldn't it be a bit irreverent not to note this occasion? After all they'd been through? At last, they were here. Here! They had arrived at an entrance. Most definitely, a celebration of some sort was called for.

"A reconnoitre, what?" Streak queried. "For just a tick?"

Agnes readily agreed. "Yes, Streak! Let's savour this grand moment!"

"Why don't we make camp and stay the night?" ChiChi suggested.

As one, they proclaimed this idea brilliant, and a small fire was set in front of the splendid archway. While dinner cooked, each pilgrim approached the gate individually. Damp cat noses snuffled its shadowy perimeter, G mimicked the many dances intricately carved onto its walls, and little girl fingers smoothed over its cool stones. Elegant and highly ornate, it was simply the most spectacular structure Agnes had ever experienced. Her heart was completely full.

Dinner enjoyed, satisfied, the group lounged around the fire, staring sleepily into its glow as the flames faded to embers. Admiring eyes lifted, following the imposing gateway upward. Storeys and storeys tall, the gate narrated its carved tales into the evening sky, inspiring ChiChi with yet another great idea.

"A story! A story!" ChiChi clamoured. Streak purred approval.

Agnes joined in. "Oh yes! Please, G! Won't you tell us a bedtime story?"

Finder settled quietly at Agnes's feet, and her small hand reached to scratch the top of his head. His eyes closed at the deliciousness of being rubbed in this special spot that few could ever reach, and he readied himself for one of G's entertaining tales. A peerless storyteller, G was always delighted to spin a fantasy for his friends.

"Shall I tell you a tale of the gods?" G asked, laying the groundwork. "A tale of creativity?" Clearing his throat, he launched into his enchantment:

"Brahma, the god of all creation, and Vishnu, the energy that sustains the universe, stood with Shiva, indulging in a game of one-upmanship. Responsible for every transformation upon which evolution depends, Shiva, of course, felt his role was the most valuable.

"'Fiddle-faddle!' Brahma exclaimed. 'Nothing could ever have happened without me,' he boasted. 'All is born from my mind. Without me, there'd be nothing!'

"Swiftly, Vishnu scoffed. 'As the in-dwelling light, without me, everything would have disappeared long ago. I keep it all going!'

"With a little trick Kali had shown him, Shiva stuck out his tongue, emitting a rather rude, 'PTHHHT!' Ever ready to up the stakes to a gamble, he continued to promote his own position. 'Wanna bet?! I am the affirmation of everything, and without me, nothing would change! Then where would we be? Have you considered *that?*'

"Round and round, they argued, going nowhere, as disagreements so often do. Each august deity puffed out his divine chest in turn, grabbing the floor to explain why he—and he alone—was the most valuable of all the gods.

"Into the midst of their squabble—right into the very centre of their argument—a tremendous basket made of sparkling gemstones descended from the sky. So immense was the basket! So scintillating its jewels! It was so full of colour and light that a great rainbow reflected from its surface, arcing into the far distance.

"Interrupting the fervour of their rebuttals, all three deities clamoured with curiosity into the basket, irresistibly drawn by its shimmering surface. Once they'd settled, the basket lifted from the ground. Up and up, it floated . . . up and over its own self-born rainbow—like a great, glowing, astral orb of a balloon." At this reference, G shared a flagrant wink with Agnes, then continued his story:

"'Look, look, look!' the great gods exclaimed, pointing to the splendour of the land as it disappeared below.

"'Look, look, look!' they cried out, as jagged snowy peaks gave way to mountains of cloud, massive thunderheads roiling into the sky. Up, up, up, they flew in the bejewelled basket, until finally, night lowered its sooty curtain, and the stars in the wide heavens sparked.

"They passed subtle universes of possibilities never before glimpsed. 'Look, look, look!' the three gods whispered as they rose, awed by the miracle of each celestial realm.

"As it neared a planetary surface, the travelling basket hesitated above the ground like a hummingbird, then lowered to an open field of light.

"Out climbed the three gods, intent on exploring the exquisite, energetic glow surrounding them. Each swooned in rapture. In his intoxicated state, Brahma stumbled and found that he had tripped over an immense, luminous foot. Recognition came to him in an instant!

"To the other gods, he recounted a time when—lost in his own dreams, lost within himself—the Earth Goddess had sidled up to him, a mischievous smile on her lips. Casting a sidelong glance his way, and raising one of her delicate eyebrows, she had delivered all the encouragement Brahma needed. Stimulated by Earth's sweet flirtation in the midst of his internal reveries, he had manifested the entire universe. His excited activity had then startled the dreaming Vishnu, who awoke in order to care for this new world.

"As Brahma recalled the initiation of his own creative act, he realized that it was this supreme goddess who had been the impetus of that creation. Without Earth, he would still be asleep, lost in his dream—as would Vishnu. Shiva too understood the implication of Brahma's recollection: it was the generative action of this divinity that had truly birthed the world, and his participation in its evolution was supported by her creative power.

"The incomparable value of relationship was the understanding reached by the three great gods; the gifts they'd deemed their own were in truth founded in interaction. The immensity of the energy that surrounded them, that permeated them . . . this was the very light that had initiated all life, that sustained all life, that evolved all life. Not one of them held more value than the other! Instead, it was within participation, within collaboration, within relationship, that brilliance had formed, and then formed again."

G interrupted his narrative to clarify the teaching hidden within his tale. "The stories of the gods are always our own stories," he reminded his friends. "'Once upon a time' is always right now. Let us take a trip to our own celestial realms, as the basket of gems is like our own bodies, glimmering with rainbows of skills, experiences, and sensations. We must climb within to recognize them."

Smiling at his friends, he urged them. "Come with me."

creativity's meditation
a practice

"For a day and a night, I travelled through the air,
and on the morning of the second day, I awoke and found
the balloon floating over a strange and beautiful country."

- L. FRANK BAUM

G eagerly guided them on his suggested journey. "Close your eyes. Settle with your breath." He let the group quiet themselves as the great gateway loomed above them, its shadow dark against the winking stars.

"Let's enjoy a ride in honour of creativity in the bejewelled 'basket' of our bodies. Let's dream ourselves into the sky. Keep the sensation of Earth beneath you, supporting you. Lay heavily upon her."

Each friend melted more fully into the softness of the forest undergrowth. "Tethering ourselves to that groundedness, we'll lift on our exhalations. Breathe out slowly, imagining a slow ascension. Feel the lift within. Your spine elongates as you inhale and creates a more spacious circumference."

After a long moment, he spoke again. "Imagine the land below you—the land you love—extending to the horizon in all directions. Witness Earth's magnificence. She spreads out below, vast and encompassing—all the green forests through which we have walked; the blue of the wild sea we have glimpsed from afar; the white-topped mountains that ring the distance."

The friends sighed as beauty overflowed their imaginations and escaped slowly on prolonged exhalations. They sensed their bodies as the glimmering colours G described.

"Inhale," G reminded them. "Find yourself in the prismatic basket of your body. Exhale easefully now. Relax yourself more deeply to lift further . . . further into the wide umbrella of sky. We pass pale, vaporous clouds. We pass the welcome heat of a golden sun. Breathe consistently. Breathe quietly.

"As you continue to rise, you lift up, up, up into space," G reiterated, "away from the sun. Further . . . further into the open air." As the companions travelled through the ether, they envisioned the darkness under their lids as the midnight sky. "Admire the constellations glinting in this indigo . . . Admire the diffuse light of the moon, shining, eternally shining . . .

"Inhale your own multicoloured inner universe. With each exhale, continue up, up, up, passing unimagined worlds of beauty and delight. With each inhale, let's appreciate our bodies for their own miracles—our senses feeding us all the colours, all the smells, all the flavours of the world around us."

Patiently, G unfurled his guidance, allowing each of the group to fully experience their own vision. "Enter now into a luminous expanse. Sense brightness under your eyelids, washing across their expanse, a glow that envelops you. We arrive now at the light-filled world of the Goddess of

Creation. We enter her universe to explore the field of our own creativity, the boundless field where potential's wellspring is revealed."

The forest breathed quietly with the pilgrims; its usual night sounds muted as the friends focused inward. "Can you sense the effulgence of your creativity pervading you? Can you feel its warm illumination emanating from the centre of your body, emanating through your pores?

"Know that this light remains ever within you, within the basket of your body. The jewels are your senses, your memories, your actions. The choices you make reflect the light of those jewels as your own rainbow—a full spectrum of influence, shining out into the world." Subtle smiles formed on the faces of the pilgrims as they felt their uplifted hearts.

"Now inhale and ride your breath back down, deeper . . . deeper . . . into your body. Draw the light within. Feel its warmth. Its glow." Quiet breathing filled the forest.

"Can you feel the light of your friends as well . . . as we share this connection?" G asked quietly. "The luminosity seeping out of their bodies? This mutual warmth, this shared light . . . this is the light of community. We might call it brainstorming. Participation. Mutual support and appreciation. Or—as our friend Krishna suggests—we might simply call it love.

"Take a few more breaths," G said, the exercise slowly reaching its conclusion. "This movement of breath rejuvenates. Your cells communicate. Your energy awakens. Softly open your eyes now and re-experience the world around you."

At this, the companions yawned, stretched, and gradually emerged from their inner journeys, each a little brighter . . . each a little lighter.

"We read the signs. We listen for the Muse," G said, summing up his tale. "And if we pay attention, one day . . . Creativity visits us. She shares an idea . . . maybe a vision or a thought. Know that this is not a simple gift!

"Creativity initiates a relationship. She asks, 'Will you meet me?' Inspiration arises from within us only as we engage— that engagement is key. Creativity is not passive. To her, we must say a resolute, 'YES!' We must treat her gift with care, cultivating it with our own attention."

Agnes blushed as she considered the many times she had squandered an idea, allowing her focus to be swayed. How rude! She would never do that again!

"Our inner worlds are given shape by our actions—in the art we generate, the words we use, the choices we make . . . in the very lives we live! Our responsibility then, in full participation with this creative process, is to share our gifts. To give our ideas life, we must share them with others."

The friends looked from G to one another, their eyes tender with gratitude.

"In this way," G concluded, smiling back at them, "we all share the sweetness of evolution. We all make more. This . . . *this* is the magic of community."

14
rest

"Rest and be thankful."

- WILLIAM WORDSWORTH

rest

Once inside the Temple's great gateway, the meandering path snaked occasionally through oceans of tall grasses, hisssssing in the most disconcerting way. Secret alleys through the forest were exposed, then just as suddenly, collapsed and closed. Another dead end. The dense canopy would crack to a slice of sky as open as a revelation, and G would look up, adjust bearings, then forge onward. These many landscapes they traversed—rocky knolls, marshy lowlands, steep cliffs, and their analogous valleys—all yielding their own treasures. Higher ground offered a welcome vantage to measure the upcoming distance. Valleys carried a cozier microclimate, in the calm comfort of which considerations drifted inward, encouraging dreams and introspection. Each was shelter—each was home—to so many diverse lives.

In her deep pockets, Agnes stashed an accumulation of feathers, pebbles, and other treasures, material memories of the various paths they walked. A shimmering beetle carcass, a fragile dragonfly wing, a bone bleached as white as the moon . . . all the sweet miracles she found underfoot. Favourite finds were seed pods: innocuous and nearly impermeable. Yet inside? Obscured within each inky interior hid all the necessary intelligence to blossom into the fullness of the plant's potential. Who isn't amazed by the magic of an entire oak tree concentrated into an acorn the size of a fingertip?

Kicking at the dirt and grasses beneath her feet, Agnes spied the convolutions of a tiny shell upon the trail. She was nonplussed. The location of the Temple's deep interior remained elusive, and she glanced over one shoulder, looked the other way, then questioned her friends, "Could we be near the sea?" The group massed about her, inquisitive of this latest clue.

From the branches overhead, they heard . . . a giggle?!

Craning their necks, its source remained obscured until the chortles became so uncontrolled that—

CRAAAACK!

—and from the limb above, sprawling and sputtering, a body fell to the ground.

Now it was G's turn to laugh, and he did so fully, his great belly heaving.

Propping himself on a somewhat bruised elbow, Vishnu narrowed his eyes at G, and in a scathing voice, inquired, "Are you quite finished?!"

But G was not, and his tummy continued to ripple and roll, convulsing in delight at the dismay so evident on Vishnu's face.

"Fancy meeting you here, Vishnu. What's up? Not you!" G tittered at his own bad joke.

With a valiant attempt to regain his dignity, Vishnu stood. Brushing himself off, he proclaimed with a regal air, "I have taken many forms in my adventures through eternity. No one knows better than I that, sometimes, we must shift course and try another way. So, I too have come to offer aid to those who seek the Lost Temple. Will you accept my help?" Palm met palm at his heart then, and he bowed.

Agnes returned his greeting, asserting herself in an attempt to defuse the silly spat between G and this Shining One. "We do seem to have hit an impasse, sir, and of course, your suggestions would be most welcome." She turned a stink eye to G, who simply winked back at her, continuing to chuckle.

Somewhat assuaged, Vishnu began to speak. "Time unfurls herself like a seashell, hence the small symbol I dropped on your path." His arm waved in a whorl, circling again each time larger, then larger still, inscribing a corkscrew in the humid afternoon air. "I myself never leave home without my own *Panchajanya* to accompany and remind me of this very fact." A shaft of sunlight pierced the forest, reflecting its brilliance off the great conch shell Vishnu held high.

"In the All Time's many recursive moments, I have entered, then re-entered, this world," he continued. His fingers drew their attention to the dotted nodes that circumscribed the shell's helix. "And I have answered to many names."

"Yes, yes," the little girl repeated, a bit impatiently. (Gosh, they didn't all have multiple lifetimes to squander!) "Indeed, we do seem to continue going in circles these last days."

The group mumbled in agreement.

"But can you suggest a remedy, sir?" Agnes asked. "What is it you do when caught in a loop?"

"Of course! Of course!" Vishnu nodded his head and got right to the point. "A good rest—that is what's needed! I always like to sleep on things."

At this statement of the obvious, G could contain his mirth no longer, and dropping to the ground, he snorted and sniggered through the expanse of his sinuously curved trunk.

Vishnu frowned. *Really?!* "PFFFTH!," the Great One raspberried through his lips, slightly put off. Still, he persevered. (What else would he do?)

"I can teach you to maximize your rest," Vishnu offered, deciding to take the higher ground and ignore the overly jovial G. "Then you too may achieve the same creative result as I. You may float upon the same sea of possibilities. And from this rest, with the simplicity of only a small offering, you will find that fresh ideas emerge without effort."

Agnes's eyes remained full of questions.

"You will make an offering of Beauty!" Vishnu elucidated. "I will show you how to descend into your own forgotten depths, the well of resources that all beings have within, shared by all life—those before you, as well as all those who will follow. Everyone has access to this source. Gather something that is of value to you and sit yourselves down. Set your offering before you. I will lead. And together, we will find our way inside."

Vishnu's meditation
a practice

"Attention is the rarest and purest form of generosity."
– SIMONE WEIL

The friends curved around this Luminous Being, placing their small treasures on the ground at their feet, then listened intently to Vishnu's directions.

"You have touched this place before, of course, in your dreams," Vishnu explained. "But just as each wave merges back into the ocean, it is always ephemeral and cannot be held but for a moment or two before it begins to dissolve. Instead, we will need to find our way to the third world— the world beyond waking, the world beyond dreaming. In this dreamless land, we will locate the field where all the Shining Ones look down upon you, watch over you—for in this state, you are in *our* world, you are in *our* dreams.

"I will show you how to lift a mirror within your mind, enabling you to gaze through the eyes of the gods and see as they see when they observe you. This is the skill that is needed to bring what you witness in the dreamless state back into your waking time."

This extravagant idea ensnared everyone's imagination, and all honoured Vishnu with the fullness of their attention.

"In the dreamless world, we are saturated in the reservoir of all experience," Vishnu continued. "Accessed again when awake, we may then draw our choices from this expansive pool of imagination. Make your own offering! Float upon this sea of recollection, buoyant on the waves of memories . . . of stories. Past and present form a continuum. This is how I dream the world into reality! This is how I manifest desire into form! Are you willing?"

Heads of all shapes and sizes nodded an emphatic yes. They all wanted tickets on Vishnu's wild oceanic ride!

"Are you comfortable?" Vishnu inquired. With his direct gaze, he invited each of the pilgrims in turn. Smiling back, they offered him their trust. "Be certain that you are. It will prove vital to your journey." His admonishment instigated a little more squirming as each found a more settled place.

"Let your lids soften until your eyes are neither open nor closed. Find them as night, as well as day. In shadowed light then, we will move into the darkness slowly. Very slowly. With eyes half open, half closed, we descend to the depths of beauty. Here we dive into the full potential of our own offerings." Buoyed on the rhythm of his speech, eyelids drooped sleepily. Skin and fur, hide and fleece all eased. Bodies expanded and contracted like waves cresting on the shore, then receding.

Cradling a shimmering disc, Vishnu leaned in and arranged it lovingly at the centre of the group. "Let your soft gaze fall upon my *Sudarshana*, the Sweetly-Seen," he said, introducing them to his discus. "Keep watch as she spins, spins, spins to clear your vision. Of course, the world is dizzying.

Its pandemonium never ceases. Resting here in meditation, we suspend ourselves within a hesitant moment to enter that very process of infinite unfolding."

With the ever-turning Earth holding them, the companions confidently sat more deeply. Their breathing coordinated. Under lowered lids, all eyes rested on Vishnu's brightly spinning wheel. "She spins. She spins. She always spins," Vishnu repeated hypnotically.

After a few quiet minutes, in a tone as liquid as the endless sea itself, Vishnu spoke again. "Court your imagination! Feel your breath exit as if only through your right nostril. Breathe out slowly. Let it enter your left nostril, inhaling equally slowly. Exhale as if just through the right side.

"Inhale as if through the left." The companions breathed along with his instructions. "Exhale as if through the right.

"Exhale, sun sets. Inhale, moon rises." In his mesmerizing cadence, Vishnu coaxed them further within. "Exhale, sun sets. Inhale, moon rises.

"Feel the lift, the fall. The lift, the fall. Feel it in your belly, as well as at your back. Feel it all around your chest as a circumferential movement.

"Sun sets. Moon rises. Exhale. Inhale."

And in this held moment, the pilgrims felt their joy within swell, mimicking the expansion of their bodies. The companions breathed as one, yet *Sudarshana* wheeled each a revelation that belonged to no one else. They watched *Sudarshana*, yes, but as they looked, they were also seen— the shining discus mirroring back their inner worlds, spinning a fractal explosion of all their latent possibilities. Off the glowing edge of the discus, prisms of colour shot in every direction, beaming small rainbows onto the leaves and branches of the forest.

Vishnu's voice joined them again. "Retain your easy eyes, your broad brow . . . Exhale. Inhale. Freely and simply. Sun sets. Moon rises. As the movement of the cosmos itself, you are in no rush. Everything has its time. Sun sets. Moon rises."

In the depths of the forest . . . in the speckled light of its leafy canopy . . . in the moist-scented tropical air . . . surrounded by the chirps and twitters of birds of all colours . . . in the fine company of friends . . . in this very precious now . . . they breathed . . . and they dreamed. They dreamed with the eyes of the Shining Ones, their world illuminated with memory's light.

"Exhale, sun sets. Inhale, moon rises. Rest against the wave of your breath . . . for you sleep now on my own infinite ocean," Vishnu whispered. "Sleep. Sleep and dream, dear ones."

And so it was that, on a river of song, on the redolent fragrance of flowers and soil, with their own treasured objects set to view, inhabited by the waving rhythm of their companions' breath, the travellers inquired after their own secreted wisdom. Conjuring the unknown through shadow and play, they listened to the worlds within with open hearts. Thoroughly enchanted, they re-emerged just as Vishnu had suggested they would: with a renewed clarity of purpose as fresh as a bluebird sky.

Rested.

waxing half moon

15

transformation

"Quiet the restlessness of the mind.
Only then will you witness everything unfolding from
emptiness."

- LAO TZU

transformation

Agnes offered encouragement as her friend worked. "Just a bit higher . . . A bit, a bit . . . A bit higher! Strrrrrrreeetch!" Finder jacked up his neck, and like a dappled ballerina, boosted himself en pointe. The travellers huddled close, supportive, ready for his report.

"Hrrummpf!" Spindly legs plicating like a fan, down the giraffe toppled. "Nope. Can't do it."

ChiChi and Streak ascended to the parapet, but their view was hindered by the expanse of densely tangled foliage. "Only bits 'n' bobs visible, I'm afraid," apologized the tiger. Like a tremendous parasol, the canopy spread as far as they could see to the left and equally far to the right. Arching branches and knotted roots crept over, under, around the perimeter walls, an arboreal exoskeleton, obscuring the way and impeding an approach to the heart of the Lost Temple.

Brows creased. Lips puckered. The group was stymied.

"Try again!" they clamoured. Gamely, the giraffe did—straining and craning, telescoping his elongated body, finally lifting extra-high onto the tippiest of tiptoes.

"Hrrummpf!" Again, he crumpled to the ground. Studying the disappointed faces of his friends, he made a decision.

In his elongated intonation, he drawled, "Okaaay, that's it—here goes!" All eyes questioned his nervousness, then blinked wide in astonishment as their long-long-long friend, this extraordinarily tall fellow, began to shrink. And shrink. And shrink. Until finally, he stood no taller than the little Canadian girl.

"W-Wow!" Agnes sputtered. "Th-tha-that was sooo cool!" On the heels of G's display of his multiple heads, the remarkable transformation of her companion was still quite overwhelming. Indeed, so unexpected was this demonstration of Finder's unknown talents that she truly hesitated to critique. Still, it needed to be said. "Unfortunately, though, you are kind of headed in the wrong direction, aren't you, sweet friend? You couldn't possibly get taller instead?" she asked hopefully.

The giraffe smirked, not yet finished with his metamorphosis. Soon, smooth jig-sawed skin became flocculent and pale, his legs squat, thick and supple, his jawline strong. And . . . Was that the hint of a beard?! With the transition complete, he let out a mighty "WHOOOP!!!" that sang through the roof of the jungle. It echoed through the branches, reverberating with the uplifting sound of unleashed joy.

Astounded, the group stared as their formerly lanky companion—now a hunkering silver simian—stooped at their feet. This lustrous ape placed palm to palm over his heart and dropped his beard to his chest. After honouring their stupefaction, he looked back up with a sly grin.

"Why . . . Is this your true form, friend?" Agnes asked.

"Hmmm . . ." the argentine ape considered her question, chewing a bit on his response. "Do we have a true form?" Finder queried back finally. "All things come, as all things go. Things that are real, remain real. One form simply becomes another. Do we not have as many faces as we choose to inhabit? Trust me—I am still the friend you know. Now watch!"

And with one frolicsome vault, he grasped a low bough, and swinging hand over hand, howling and flipping, scampering and hooting, he traversed the canopy. His eureka resounded back to his travel mates: "I see it! I see the golden rooftop of the Lost Temple!" Romping back down from his reconnaissance, he stood triumphant in their joy.

"I wish I could see it too!" Deep desire ached in the little Canadian girl. The approach inside the great gateway had been arduous, with the Temple's centre—like a secret tightly held—still eluding them. Anxious too for a glimpse of their destination, the pilgrims all murmured sympathetically.

"Take a seat," suggested the silver shapeshifter, "and we will share a practice. Then, I assure you, we will *all* see the inner heart of the Lost Temple."

transformation's meditation
a practice

"Dwell on the beauty of life.
Watch the stars and see yourself running with them."

– MARCUS AURELIUS

Curving into a small circle on the forest floor, the comrades listened attentively to the simian's instructions:

"Soften your gaze . . .
watch only the light flickering through the leaves . . .
silver light . . .
like moonlight on my lustrous fur . . ."

A gentle gust rustled a whisper through the grasses nearby.

"Feel the breeze . . .
cool on your skin . . .
Let it pass freely . . .
as if through you . . .
permeating your pores . . .
Follow it . . ."

The friends felt their thoughts carried along on a voice as silken as that wind, as the shapeshifter continued his intonation:

"The light is free . . . free movement . . .
gentle . . . so gentle . . .

See the pattern of the light through the leaves . . .
just the light . . . just the pattern . . .
It shapes itself . . . has its own form . . ."

The silver simian repeated:

"Just the light . . . just the light . . .
Watch the shape as it shifts . . . as it forms, forms
again . . .
shifts . . . shifts again . . .
It moves, it moves, always moves . . . the same, yet
constantly changing . . .
flickering, focusing . . . shifting, changing . . .
Hold the light in your eyes . . . this pattern of light . . .
Your eyelids become heavy . . . heavy . . .
close of their own accord . . .
Listen . . ."

Finder was silent as the wind ruffled leaves, brushed skin
and fur. He stayed quiet, as birds trilled and whistled, quiet,
as water nearby burbled, soothed over rocks.

Again, he led the group back into the forest's senses:

"Feel the breeze . . . on your skin . . . cool . . .
Hear it . . . hear it . . .
Allow silence to find you . . . leave you . . . then find
you again . . .
Remember the light's pattern . . .
See it now . . . in your mind's eye . . .
It moves . . . it moves . . . always moves . . .
The sound moves too . . . moves within you . . ."

His voice slowed, softening to a shining whisper:

> "The pattern shifts . . . flickers . . .
> The light moves . . . The wind moves . . .
> The sounds change . . . the sounds change . . ."

Adrift on the rich timbre of their old friend's new voice, the hearts of the pilgrims lifted and fell in rhythm with the easy breeze:

> "It all moves . . .
> It all moves . . .
> always moves . . ."

Their breath rose, carrying them aloft through the forest on waves of chittering birdsong. Caressed by a cool breeze, their bodies rooted down into the embrace of the Earth. Behind closed eyes, dappled patterns of light formed and reformed, creating fresh shapes. Inside this treasured space of participation, their many hearts found a single rhythm as the travellers witnessed the true gift of deep friendship: a shared dream . . . a shared vision.

16

earth

"There are only two ways to live your life.
One is as though nothing is a miracle.
The other is as though everything is a miracle."

- ALBERT EINSTEIN

earth

G was reflective, as he and his friends lay below a generous green canopy, grateful for its wide shadow. "This tree . . . this sumptuous, incomparable tree. I know her well."

With the air in the forest ponderous and humid, the shadow of this immense tree was indeed a gift, her flourishing boundless as she stretched a convoluted network of swelling growth across the forest floor. Connecting back to Earth again and again, her many branches rooted and re-rooted to shore her abiding stability. All had felt immediately at home, settling comfortably to enjoy the hospitality of her shade. Entranced by her animated play of light, they gazed into the complexity of her branches as—ruffled by the warm winds—her leaves alternately sparkled and shadowed, sparkled and shadowed.

Agnes turned slowly to G, his words cracking into her developing wariness. *He knows this tree?! How? Just what is going on here?* Her brow puckered deeply as Agnes speculated. What had really happened to G—or more to the point—what was continuing to happen to him? More arms. More girth. Admittedly, he had developed some spectacular abilities, as she recollected G's spinning of his one head into five. He'd always been smart, but now he was terribly smart. Smarter than ever.

He was still her old friend, and yet he held memories for which Agnes couldn't account, like his acquaintance with many of the miraculous beings they were encountering. *Had he travelled this way on his solo walkabout? Holy smoke— is he continuing to transform?!* The idea was dizzying. Of course, G would say they were all continuing to evolve, and certainly, that was something she couldn't argue.

There was something more, though, something intangible about their most erudite member. Once or twice, he seemed about to share something, but . . . Agnes sighed. As billed, this journey certainly was proving mysterious!

G furthered his telling: "The seed for this tree was poured from the sky on the River of Stars. She represents persistence given form and is one of our Most Ancients."

"Even older than you, G?" ChiChi teased.

"In my new form, you may think I am old," G replied, uncharacteristically sombre. "But this tree is a being much older still, my friend. She is the Green Mother of us all, one with the very Earth. She breathes life. And under her verdant umbrella—this verdant womb—we all find our place."

Decidedly intrigued, Agnes encouraged G to continue. Streak lifted a drowsy head from his incessant grooming, and the silver ape descended from the branching canopy to hear more.

"Her courage is without limit, and she holds many universes. Righteous battles that last tens of thousands of years are waged within her arms. Still, she endures." Grandly, G unfurled the story of the Ancient One. "Durga, Kali, Shri— all the Shining Lights of Power abide within her, for it is this Green Mother who sustains them, just as she sustains us all."

In acknowledgement of G's respect, shimmering leaves fluttered, allowing golden light to shaft through the forest.

"Is the air not more redolent, more gratifying here in her shade?" G posed. The group inhaled deeply, and simultaneously exclaimed:

"Catnip!"

"Banana!"

"Fish tails!"

"Orange blossoms . . . or wait . . . rose petals?"

Catnip and fish and flowers?! Utterly flummoxed, eyes wide, they looked to their wise friend as G explained. "From seed spilled down on moonlight's pale liquidity, the Tree of the World was birthed from the Milky Way. She listens as we whisper our deep desires, as we all have aspirations, special yearnings to seek out and fulfill. And since we each hope for something different, something our own, she offers each a scent that pleases, satisfying those desires. It is comforting, is it not, to have someone with whom to share our dreams? A place to go where we will be heard and encouraged? A being who welcomes us as consistently and fully as any mother because she IS our mother?

"As one of our Most Ancients, her roots stretch into eternity, creating the architecture for all those who live on this Earth. She is our literal support. And as the witness to our dreams—hopes both fulfilled and discarded—her memories are all memories. From the very depths of her organic being, all life thrives, all form emerges, all possibilities manifest."

Tenderly, G explained the inestimable preciousness of the Tree of the World. "In her eternal expansion, freely she offers her beneficence. She makes herself a gift as the source of all potential."

As G spoke the story of the Green Mother, the sun set. Now a buoyant half-moon filtered her intimate light through the boughs of the Ancient One. Twinkling orbits broke through dense foliage, creating wondrous starbursts, swirling nebulae, and speeding comets on the ground around them. Infinite lights danced for each of the infinite small galaxies of desire animating under fallen fronds and broken twigs, on moss and under stone—the constancy of heartbeats-beats-beats in every unbroken moment under her umbrageous sky.

The companions listened to the crawling and scrabbling, slithering and squirming—all the many lives amongst the mountains and hollows of the Green Mother's great arboreal cosmos. The blurred goodnight prayers of a fur-soft bee. A lonely cicada's first chirp. The wet slap of tree frog meeting leaf. "Hoo-hoo-hoo-hooo," an owl echoed.

The hum of the pilgrims' attention translated light's language into a multitude of wee altars, all surrendering to this green epiphany—to all the possibilities pulsing within the Green Mother's exuberant foliage.

17
confidence

"To be yourself in a world that is
constantly trying to make you something else
is the greatest accomplishment."

- RALPH WALDO EMERSON

confidence

S treak and ChiChi caught an odour on the wind. True to his name, like a streak, the tiger was off to investigate, with ChiChi left to guard the group. Another great cat was in proximity.

"ROARRR!" Fat and throaty, Streak rumbled the all-clear, and soon the pilgrims found him—as golden fur entwined shadowed stripes—tumbling and licking, rolling and purring with not one but two silken lions. Grand and glorious in her prowess, the mighty warrior Durga stood by, smiling as her mount and the second lion frolicked with Streak.

"I'm so glad you found us!" G touched a grateful hand to his brow, to his lips, then to his heart.

Okay, that's it! Agnes thought. *There's something no end of odd about my G.* She was soon to find out just what that was, as the goddess returned G's greeting.

"Aho' Simha Ganapati!" Durga called.

"HOLY SMOKE! Ganapati?!!" Agnes squeaked. G turned to her and bowed. "I knew something was up!" In her surprise, her voice pitched high, Agnes took in this confirmation of G's radical transformation. Small stuffed· elephant had become an elephant-headed boy. Then her G had gone walkabout and re-emerged a Great Being. Now Agnes understood the fullness of G's miraculous change: illuminated by his own inner light, he had become a Shining One.

Durga interrupted her incredulity. "I have delivered your mount, Ganapati, for it is time to ascend your own lion. On this final leg of the journey you have undertaken, the threats are many. To complete your quest will require the full courage of your huge heart."

Beautiful and bedecked in fine armour, her gaze tranquil, Durga's clipped enunciation revealed her martial training— as did her taut physique. Mirroring her lion mount, she herself was feline, her powerful body rippling with sinuous muscle. Intelligent eyes captured the wide scene, yet indicated no judgement, no concern. One could not read her thoughts. And while she stood calmly, it was evident to all that she was ever ready to answer the call to action.

The little Canadian girl was mesmerized.

Acknowledging this admiration, Durga took Agnes aside. "There is no doubt that I train hard, little one. I am always prepared—in body as well as in heart. This is one key to power, Agnes: lay the groundwork by practicing your skills assiduously. Life can be challenging—no one will argue that. But don't get lost in your preparations, for they are only that. There is a time for training, yes. Foundation is forged in discipline. But when it is time to act, the drills are over. Practice is over. Act! Be confident that you will draw from the resources you have honed."

Agnes appreciated Durga's candidness. Her small chin dropped in humility, faced with the palpable integrity of this enduring goddess.

"However," Durga continued, turning back to address the whole group, "I do have a secret to my invincibility. And I have come to share it with those who seek the Lost Temple."

Excitement sparking in her eyes, Agnes held her breath and listened with her entire being. She wanted so much to learn from this remarkable female.

"It is deceptive in its simplicity," Durga prefaced, then offered a warning, "but simple does not mean easy. Remain composed! This is my secret. The difficulties faced—demons from within and without—all will underestimate you. Indeed, you might even underestimate yourself."

At this, Durga levelled her direct gaze at Agnes, choosing her words with precision. "Know your value! All will see you as slight. Just a little girl. Perhaps this is even how you see yourself. Expose this vulnerability! Advantage is found in the weakness of prejudice. There you will find susceptibility. Meet that frailty with the very strength of who you are."

The great goddess fixed her eyes back on Agnes. She recognized that the little girl was as yet unconvinced of her own capacity.

"AGNES! Hear me!" Durga insisted, then repeated her clear counsel: "Know your value! Your experiences are your training. Draw from this source. You must believe in your ability. In your power. You must believe that you hold the resources to meet any challenge. Trust yourself first! Act as you know to be right. To be true. Then, even if you falter, you will have done your best. And this is all we can ask of ourselves—and of others."

Agnes felt the fine words of the deity fill her up. She stood taller. Lifting her chin, she nodded slowly, then ventured a question: "You have so many weapons, Durga. Maybe I need a weapon as well?"

Agnes had always favoured the crossbow . . . or perhaps a ninja star? She considered the goddess's mount . . . Maybe she needed her own well-trained familiar? (A bee? Yes, just her size! And a bee would prove a potent, if unexpected, partner.)

As if she'd heard Agnes's inner musings, the Shining One smiled down at the gameness of this little girl. "My own invincibility pervades you," Durga assured Agnes unambiguously. "You need only hold the commitment of your own worth! Demons of insecurity, of envy, of ignorance—these are ever ready to attack. Meet them. Meet them with the tools already at hand: optimism, confidence, and compassion. These are your weapons, Agnes! Patience. Knowledge. Curiosity. You possess weapons aplenty!"

Durga's voice was calm, her strategy explicit. "Make room within yourself for the fullness of your experience. Make room for the demons too, Agnes," Durga counselled. "For they will surely come! Apathy will slay your heart if you allow its indifference to convince you. At an inappropriate time, anger will sever your will more surely than the point of a dagger. Do not shirk from the demons; do not hide. Know them! Know them as yourself. Only then will your combat become real. Only then will victory be yours."

With ferocity, Durga spun her multiple arms into a shiny blur of blades and sharpened prods. "Retain your passion, Agnes! Do not waver!"

Steel filled the forest with its metallic whirring, until the indomitable goddess abruptly halted, pointing her three-pronged *trishula* deliberately. "Follow this path! Continue until you reach another of the Elder Trees. As is customary, stop to honour her divinity. Then an abrupt turn to the east! Soon you will find an opening to the Lost Temple's deep interior."

Frankly, at this point in their long journey, Agnes was quite content to receive such forthright instructions. Sometimes, we all just need a little navigational aid to set us on the right road.

18

abundance

"Who are the gods?
The gods are who you are, who you want to be,
what you can be, what you could be."

- DOUGLAS R. BROOKS

16

abundance

What I wanted
I had always received, and now, so well that I
knew the world's abundance

—DOUGLAS R. BROOKS

abundance

B ack on the forest path, the deep woods flanking it were full of the usual nightly harmonies. Flapping, whirring, murmuring—the forest never silent. Astride his colossal lion, G had taken the lead, with ChiChi and Streak now guarding the rear.

From one of G's many hands, a great whorled shell appeared. Hoisting it to his mouth, inflating plump cheeks, G bleated a tremendous vibration into the air, a din which shook the branches above them. Within moments, a responding bugle rippled forth—or was it two?

The sound ebbed.

Again, G trumpeted his colossal conch horn, its resonance as much felt as heard. A protracted "aummmmmmmmm" hummed out through the forest, returning to them as a wave returns.

ABUNDANCE

Again and again and again, G caused the exceptional Sound of Sounds to roam outward. Again and again and again, it echoed back. Each time, its shape subtly altered, dissolved, then restored. These reciprocating vibratory conversations ferried the group across an expanse of time and space as tremors and oscillations infiltrated their inner experience.

G's horn called. Was the answer a response? A message? Or was it a memory?

Enveloping the sounds of the forest, the hum encompassed the voices of all creatures as an orchestra draws its instruments into a symphony. Persistent and unending, its throb sparkled in the galaxies of light within their eyes, its sound seeping into their skin until the companions felt they had always been buoyed on its vast vibrational current as it sounded and resounded without end.

"This aum," G explained, "is called the *pranava*. And indeed, it is an aural memory, a coming to life, the very breath of the expanding universe celebrating itself. Its sound is with us, and within us, transporting all the potencies of consciousness."

"It sounds so . . . familiar," Agnes said hesitantly while the rest of the travellers nodded their agreement.

"Of course, it does!" G laughed. "It is the ubiquity: all sound, belonging to everyone and everything in this entire universe. You have always heard it, even if you were unaware, for it is beingness, unzipping itself in an ever-expanding ripple of energy. And as essential things do, it contains a message. Its directive? A compelling imperative expressed as an eternal exhalation—it is life's urgency calling out: 'YES! YES! YES!'"

Aummmmmmmmmm . . .

Forest path opened to glade, where they were greeted by the counterpart to G's evocation. Two enormous white elephants flanked a splendid woman, seated tall upon a lotus afloat in a large pond. Her floral throne as pinkly innocent as the flush on a child's cheeks, shimmering red silks wound her slim body, and she welcomed the friends with two arms wide, while two more arms folded gently over her heart. She was a resplendent vision of vibrancy—luscious and as sweet as a ripe fruit.

Laying their own conch horns along the shore of the pond, the moon-white elephants dipped their pallid trunks into the water and lustrated this magnificent goddess with a fresh sluice of scented water. She smiled in delight at each fresh splash—the elephants, the water, the goddess, all in an enduring act of revivification.

The companions found it effortless to return her easy warmth.

"I am Shri," she announced. "And it is my infinite joy to generate more, always more, for I am the glory of prosperity, the wealth of individual choice. I have come to offer my own boon, to share my capacity for continuous growth. I will teach you to locate advantage, to manifest bounty, as each of you is sufficient unto your own joy, just as you are sufficient unto your own needs. Will those who pursue the Lost Temple hear me?" The group gathered at her petals' edge, risking a fragrant splash, eager to share in the magic of this charismatic beauty.

Her incantation sang out: *"Yoyat icchiti tasya tat!"*

Whaaaa . . .?! All eyes turned expectantly to Ganapati, who obliged with a translation. "This is from the Upanishads," he explained, "and it means 'for each, what is desired will come.'"

Shri dipped her delicate chin in approval.

Raising two vermillion lotus buds in their honour, she tendered her gifts. "Seekers of the Lost Temple," Shri met each of the travellers with a clear gaze, "the gift I offer is a gift already given—indeed, it is a gift born within you." Wrinkled brows instantly conveyed the group's lack of comprehension.

The goddess clarified. "I could say that, to grant you valour on your quest, I award you all the strength of my elephant companions. I could say that, for you, bountiful abilities will be yours. Or perhaps, I could say that my beneficence will result in the courage to actualize any potential you possess."

"Any of those gifts would be most appreciated, Auspicious One!" Agnes agreed, as the others nodded vigorously in agreement.

This Luminous One allowed patience to help carry her point. "If I speak my words thus, would you not think it is I who holds the responsibility for their realization? That, without my words, you would have no valour, no strength, no blossoming abilities?" Brows wrinkled again, as the companions considered this conundrum.

"Instead, what I tell you—and please hear it," Shri reiterated, "is that for each, what is desired will come! You were born not for any specific purpose, but for a purpose *you* devise. And it is in the expression of that choice that you create more of yourself. So, it is you then who actually creates me." The deity giggled delightedly at her own sinuous logic.

"If you want courage, little Agnes," the goddess said, addressing the Canadian girl directly, "it will be yours. Not because I gave it to you but because you yourself gave it value, deigning it worthwhile." She paused for a moment, letting her example sink in. "If you desire strength, it awaits you, already yours. Each moment you are confronted with choice, you decide what matters, where you will expend your efforts, where you will place your attention. You and only you. This is your freedom: to choose! Or to not choose, which is in itself a choice." She laughed again, joy exuding from her every gesture.

"Please sit," Shri invited. "Let us meditate together." Friends of all shapes and sizes gathered close.

Shri's meditation
a practice

"The best and most beautiful things in the world cannot
be seen or even touched.
They must be felt with the heart."

– HELEN KELLER

Once the group had quieted comfortably, Shri began, centering her attention on the little Canadian girl:

"Turn your left palm upwards on your thigh, Agnes, your fingers gently together, your elbow close to your ribs. Now move that hand away from you, until your fingers just slide over the edge of your knee, allowing the backs of your fingers to softly drape toward the floor. This is *Varada Mudra*, the gesture of generosity," Shri demonstrated the mudra herself, her graceful fingers laid open in offering.

"I love this expansive hand gesture," the goddess murmured tenderly as Agnes settled herself and mimicked Shri. "We are creating art—a communication—with our bodies, our hands evoking tendencies, capacities, and inner possibilities, with mudra as the vessel that receives our experience. In this way, Agnes, the well-lived life, the quotidian experiences of your day, all your joys and accomplishments, are deities in the form of the world. Your hands express your purpose—a gathering of your thoughts. If you move as a god, assume the shape of a god—send your thoughts to roam the wilderness of all experience—you find then that you are the divine. So, we are not different, you and I." Shri smiled her sweetness at Agnes, and the little Canadian girl beamed back.

"To take this gesture then is to express our generous inner nature. We ask ourselves: what do we have that we can freely give? This mudra highlights our true wealth: an endless wellspring of love, of kindness, of sincerity. It demonstrates our feeling that we have enough . . . enough to share. Do you not find it a welcoming and compassionate gesture, little one?" the goddess asked, before turning to address the whole group.

"It is as if you are opening the door to your heart, then offering the best of yourself to the arriving guest."

Shri continued her gentle directions. "Take a few breaths here, to sense this gesture of giving. You can take *Varada Mudra* with your right hand as well, or rest that hand on your heart, if you prefer." The little Canadian girl slid her focus into her hands, absorbing the sensation of their positions.

"Now, for the magic." Shri winked. "Can you allow your entire body to sense this same expansive, generous quality? Use your imagination to establish your whole body as *Varada Mudra*, your whole being as a gesture of sharing your own abundant nature. What does that shape look like? Remember: you are becoming a vessel to receive experience. Prepare yourself! What slight adjustments might you make to feel abundance emanate naturally from you, with complete ease, simply from your posture? Do your shoulders widen? Does your back broaden?" Shri suggested. "Imagine yourself as a depiction of sincerity. Would you sit a little taller, perhaps more confidently in your seat?

"Now watch your breath's movement, for it is in conversation with the cosmos." The friends inhaled the scent of forest and lotus pond, and pleasure brought easy smiles to their faces.

"The universe enters you, and as you exhale, you give back some of yourself to the world around you." Shri continued her guidance, quietly yet firmly, and the companions opened themselves willingly to the goddess's words. "Is the quality of your breath affected as you feel this light of generosity flowing through you . . . flowing out into the world?

"We do our best to navigate the troubled waters of our times—our own internal trials, our personal challenges, what we struggle to understand, as well as what life unexpectedly throws our way. From simple bad luck to monumental tragedies. Remember that it is always new for all of us! Life is a process of learning, and while its glories are no doubt endless, at times, the battles can seem endless as well. Anxiety surrounds us, with much outside of our control. Fears can creep in silently and surprise us—even in our dreams." Shri's voice deepened with palpable empathy. "It is only our response to these events that is ours to adjust, only our response that is ours to adapt. Our wellness and ease become ever more vital, with reflection an oasis from the chaos.

"Can you give more of yourself to gravity? Allow yourself to feel supported. Return to a sense of your breath, gently moving. Moving, as all things must. Stay inside . . . and recognize the infinite source of wealth you hold, the beauty of your natural abundance. Inside you, all is moving too. Your feelings, your thoughts, your sensations . . . Allow the flow.

"If you take time for your own quiet contemplation, my dears," Shri said, concluding her instruction with a gentle reminder, "you will feel your perspective shift, your vision refreshed. You will find yourself revitalized in other ways as well. When we sit like this, we create a time of deep remembrance. Taking *Varada Mudra*, you tap into your internal expansive capacities, the boundless depths of your inner resources. Then you remember that all moves . . . that all *must* move. Embrace the movement. That is my teaching.

"And when we embrace movement, when we honour that shifting, then of course we recognize that truly, there is always more." The Shining One turned to address the little girl directly once again. "More capacity, Agnes. More creativity. More ideas. More possibilities. Always and always more . . ."

19

abundance, again
(there's always more)

"Illumined hearts
wake up to their own desire."

- GOPALA SUNDARAMOORTHY

abundance, again
(there's always more)

As the group opened their eyes, each indeed felt the revivification the goddess had described, their meditation like a sweet-scented splash from her pearlescent elephants. All turned to pay their respects, bowing gentle heads over gentle hearts as they faced the resplendent Shri.

Blessing them with her brilliant smile, the goddess was insistent as she assured them, "You each have everything you need. But squander it not, for you need everything you have! Spend the currency of your attention with care. Then—and only then—will you manifest what you choose to value. It is through your own engagement that what you want is made real."

Enchanted by her beauty and beguiled by her counsel, the group listened deeply. Each felt yearning surge within—motivations, inclinations, aspirations. And with Shri's encouragement, their confidence bloomed.

"What I grant you may sound straightforward—and it is," the goddess said, smiling. "My contribution is simply the contentment to recognize your own good fortune. Aptitude cares how much you care; just as in any relationship, you will be returned only what you invest. You possess skill. To fulfill it, that skill hungers for your desire. These are attributes I need not give you, as they are already yours. As I have said, what is desired will come, and when you continue to feed that desire with your effort, desire will stay. Choice is your innate gift, so consider with care."

Shri charmed the group sweetly. "So, it is genuinely gratitude then that is my offering. A deep appreciation of what you already possess is the truest gift of all."

Their audience over, Shri's lotus throne began to softly fold, enclosing her within its blushing bud as she offered them a final guidance: "May your journey bloom itself in beauty, friends, flourishing as my own eternally blossoming lotus! To find your path, follow in my steps . . . follow in my steps . . ."

Agnes pointed excitedly to the delicate impressions appearing in the grass beside them, each a tiny footprint.

Following this path of ever more, the companions wound their way deeper into the forest within the great temple complex, as the Imperishable resounded:

"Aummmmmmmmmm."

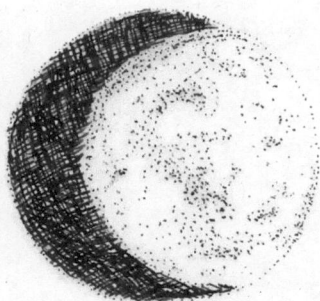

waxing gibbous

20

concealment

"All grown-ups were once children,
but only few of them remember it."

- ANTOINE DE SAINT-EXUPERY

concealment

The silver ape had transformed into a giraffe once again and stretched to the ruby fruits that dangled so invitingly overhead. Orb after pomegranate orb, Finder plucked, tossing them to his travel-mates below, who hungrily devoured each, crimson juice squirting wildly.

"HOLY SMOKE!" (Truth be told—like most of her countrymen—the little Canadian girl had a sailor's more expressive vocabulary, but this is not the place for such things.) "I was simply, utterly, and completely ravenous!" she exaggerated. "Thank you, thank you, my friend!"

"KHOT! KHOT!"

Interrupted at their fruitful feast, hearing this harsh throat-clearing hack, the pilgrims bolted upright. Syrupy red ribbons dribbled down chins, stippling a be-pocketed frock and adding extra lines to furry stripes. All were silent as full mouths hurried to swallow.

Squat and rotund, a figure stood in their midst. "KHOT! KHOT!" he coughed again, this time lifting spidery eyebrows and giving his own chin a furtive brush. Oh! Tongues of varying lengths materialized to lap up the juicy evidence.

"As I was saying," the portly man continued, once tidiness had been restored. "KHOT! KHOT!"

"Yes! Yes! We heard," G grumbled, a bit testy at his meal's postponement. "What can we do for you, my brother?" he inquired of this additional plump presence.

"I am here at the request of my wife, the Journey of Life herself. She longs for me to bestow my favours upon those who seek the Lost Temple."

Still quite peevish from hunger, G deprecated, "And your contribution is . . .?"

Not used to his offer of a gift being so ill-received, the stout man griped, "Well, I might say you're already partaking of it!" He nodded meaningfully to the preponderance of fruit peelings littering the orchard.

At this, Finder wobbled forward, folded his gangly legs, and bowed a long neck to the ground. "Oh, Protector of the World," he said, his slow intonation aiming to soothe and ingratiate. "Oh, Hero of the Earth! My friends certainly intend no dishonour. Simply, I believe, they have failed to recognize Kubera, the Lord of Hidden Treasures."

Limpid giraffe eyes rotated back to the others. "For many eons, Kubera has ruled over the riches of a splendorous golden island."

"Hmmmph. Well, fortunes do change!" Kubera shrugged, philosophically. "Not there anymore—I'm in Shiva's neighbourhood now." He jerked a thumb to the distant frosty mountains.

"Awfully sorry to hear that," Finder apologized. "Have you lost everything then?"

"Naaaah." Kubera waved off the misdeeds of the past. "It's all good! Wherever I live is a garden of wonder—wealth takes many forms. I have a wife, kids. A ton of friends!"

G took this as a cue to bring the parley back into focus. Tummies rumbled—and his own was positively deafening. "Your trees are certainly lush with sweetness, Kubera, my man." At this casual address, the Lord of Hidden Treasures winced, not at all sure this fellow G was his cup of tea. "But just what is this gift you bring?"

"The jewels that hang from my trees are treasures indeed," Kubera replied. "And you are welcome—more than welcome—to eat." G warmed. "But my boon to you is my most prodigious power. My gift is . . ." Kubera hesitated until he had achieved the desired dramatic effect, then concluded. "Concealment!"

Silence.

Big. Fat. Soft. Juicy. Silence.

A venerable old being, Kubera was much wilier than he appeared. Admittedly unassuming—stubby and hirsute— he commanded the vast original tribes of Earth and Sky. "What is hidden," he continued, expounding his argument in straightforward terms, "retains great power. It is a deep well of fortune. Note it. Claim it. Value it. It will soon prove its worth."

The companions' journey was taxing them. Though weary and hungry, they were not foolish enough to disparage aid— no matter how recondite. Kubera's strong, simple words were daunting, and they stood now in front of the Protector of the World in humility and bowed their gratitude.

"Will you sit?" Kubera invited. "Sit and eat your fill!" At this, the companions all happily dove back into their fruit-ful bounty, and when satiated, listened attentively to the advice Kubera offered.

"Desire asks us to deepen," he began. "Deepen knowledge, deepen movement . . . deepen breath, commitment, dedica-tion. Even deepen desire itself. Follow this admonishment and down the rabbit hole we go. Aimed in a single direc-tion, a linear plot that drives successive progression, we seek the continual and the consecutive.

"Imagine, instead, a pulse. A rhythm that beats with our hearts, a pulse that increases its circumference, then draws close again and again. We reach out, then return home, drawing some of the world back with us. And so, rather than deeper, consider desire's sensation as width—a wide, expansive retrieval." The friends were held rapt as, with lan-guage and intonation, Kubera wove his spell.

"Consider the enrichment of our abilities as a journey through acknowledgement and appreciation. Our breath, our bodies, our movements all draw from this open network of possibilities, tendrils of awareness emerging in every direction like a healthy root system. Exploring that spreading growth, those myriad forces rebound to restore vitality as if to a seed and embellish the context of our lives.

"Nature conceals talents within all of us, gems waiting to be 'mine'd." Kubera snickered at his pun. "Gems to make our own."

His self-amusement back under control, he continued. "Sift. Refine," he insisted. "You may have to dig—to dig deep. Are you apprehensive? Perhaps even afraid? Be well-assured: your fear won't evaporate. You can't make it disappear. No one can! For to be fearless is to be foolish! Bravery means only that you will face your fear—not that you will erase it. Joy as well does not dissolve. All these energies swirl through you and remake themselves, as the shape of clouds transform. Each energy becomes part of you, as food itself does.

"So, here's the trick!" The group leaned in, as if to taste the advice Kubera so generously imparted. "Take the energy that frightens you, that grieves you, even that disgusts you, and re-apply it, changing it into something that provides you nourishment. That feeds your ideas. That grows your motivation. Your body does this all the time! One thing becomes something else entirely. To draw your heart and thoughts into alignment with this process, become aware . . . then *participate in it.*" The pilgrims nodded, invigorated by Kubera's energy.

"The World is here. It *is*," Kubera emphasized. "Emotions are Real Things. Real Things don't disappear. But they do change—as everything does. The underlying formlessness of things shows itself in the shapeshifter. Can you master the skill?" he asked simply. "Can you penetrate it, saturating yourself in the transformation? Adroitness in this technique will aid you in ways you cannot ever foresee."

Agnes pondered this revelation. With Finder's recent illustration of his own shapeshifting, she was wont to acquire this dexterity—even if Kubera spoke of something less overt.

"Dive into emotion as the deepest pool!" Kubera advised. "Dive right into it—no matter what it is. Don't shirk or avoid it. Don't stand at its shore. Only then you will begin to recognize your own ability to reshape it. Only then will you know it as yourself.

"Consider each emotion you experience as a tool. In the right hands, at the right moment, the right tool is most useful. Employ the wrong device, though, and . . . well . . . you know." He chuckled. "Disaster! Maybe small. Maybe large. Maybe short-lived. Maybe life-altering. Who's to say? Try your best, and as a very wise man once advised, if you make a mistake, don't make it again. And if you make it again, then don't make it again." Delighting in this concise down-to-earth admonishment, Kubera laughed heartily.

"If we possess a treasure, we hold it close, do we not? Perhaps even hide it in order to protect it? I rule the Abode

of Treasures, and I tell you"—Kubera's voice lowered intimately— "my life's work is protecting that wealth. I share it
only with those I deem worthy of my gifts. This, this, this is
the value of concealment!" He rose as he spoke. Surrounded
by this small group, Kubera sighed. He did so much want to
help . . . Would they hear him? Really hear him? He could
but try . . .

Exhaling strongly, he drove his point home. "To discover
the riches you have cached at your very core, you must
spend time with yourself. To uncover is to recover! What
is of value may be hidden, but with proper attention, you
will recognize it. Then—and only then—will it truly belong
to you! You will have 'mine'd it! Enrapture yourself with
the lifting of each veil. Curiosity is the initiation. Learning
follows. The treasure is in access. And with each new discovery, the sweetness returns."

Kubera waited. The companions waited. Had the Lord of
Hidden Treasures exposed all? "That's it!" Kubera exclaimed
finally, breaking the impasse. Lifting his furry brows and
chortling at the simplicity of it all, he was off.

"Keep those sticky chins up!" he shouted back with a
final giggle.

21

imagination

"You are the secret the universe is telling."

- GOPALA SUNDARAMOORTHY

imagination

Ffffooom . . . Ffffooom . . . Ffffooom . . .

"Did you hear that?!" Agnes looked up, searching the dense foliage for a bit of open sky. Silhouetted against the blue, wide wings beat past.

"Ahhh!" G exclaimed. "That was Hamsa! We must be nearing Sarasvati's flowing waters." As usual, G was right.

Within the hour, the travellers stood on a river's downy bank, in front of the Lady herself. Wound in a gown as pale as moonlight, dipping pearly toes into the brook, Sarasvati welcomed them. The air was fresh, the water clear. Everything—including the goddess herself—scintillated. Sarasvati wore no jewels, yet she twinkled, shimmering like a star. Dazzling light was everywhere.

"Dear one!" She caught sight of Ganapati first, of course (he being the literal elephant in the room). "You've brought friends!" Extending her elegant arms to the pilgrims, Sarasvati urged, "Sit, sit!" The allure to follow the goddess's invitation was irresistible. Comfortable on a pillowy tuft of moss, Agnes settled herself.

For each of her guests, Sarasvati poured a tiny porcelain cup of a transparent liquid. "Please refresh yourselves!" As the travellers sipped, they found renewed clarity, a lucidity of thought. Eyes brightened, senses heightened, spirits revived.

Lowering her melodious voice, the cultured beauty leaned intimately toward Agnes. "You've come just in time. Hamsa and I are in the midst of a haiku recital." Directing conversation back to the group then, she said, "Hamsa, please!" She waved at him to continue.

Responding to her request, a miniature white goose—grace itself in the air—wobbled forward comically. In the clearing of his throat, he repeated his own name: "Ham-Sa." Then fixing his gaze on Sarasvati, he intoned . . .

> *"River of heaven's*
> *wide starlight spins eternal.*
> *Shared mirth beckons."*

At this recitation, the goddess clapped her hands in delight. Hamsa bowed deeply.

"Sir G?" Sarasvati arched a delicate eyebrow. "Will you play?"

Ganapati did not hesitate. "Always!" he responded, dramatically lifting his left leg to strike the artful dancer's pose. In the clearing, G's voice beamed out as a luminosity . . .

"Moonlight falling soft
frost across this water's blue.
Her ankles' small bells."

This composition too pleased the goddess. Spreading her silvery skirts like Hamsa's wings, she curtsied sweetly. "Exquisite, my radiant friend."

In her musical tones, Sarasvati now turned to address the little Canadian girl. "I too would aid those who seek the Lost Temple. I too wish to share a boon."

In anticipation, Agnes heard her own heart beating as Hamsa's powerful wings. Fffffooom! Ffffooom! Ffffooom!

"My offering is an ever-flowing river of your own—an eternal stream from the immeasurable River of Consciousness. Of course, in all honesty, this was gifted to you many years ago, coursing between the banks of possibility's infinitude and those possibilities all your own."

Flustered, Agnes shook her head. Was she mesmerized by the brilliance of this incandescent goddess? Had Sarasvati just said she'd already given her . . . a river?!

"I'm enormously g-grateful f-for your generosity," Agnes stammered in dismay. A river of her own . . . Where could she have put it?! (HOLY SMOKE! And she'd thought losing a temple was reckless!) "I'm embarrassed to say, miss, that I seem to have misplaced it. Well, actually, I didn't even know I had it!"

Sarasvati laughed easily, her eyes sparkling like starlight. As she reached a lustrous hand to Agnes, the entire forest shimmered in a vaporous mirage, then coalesced into form once again. "The river I tendered is always with you, little one—has always been with you. Insistent, it is the uninterrupted flow of your imagination. It is the questions you ask. It flows as the movement of your thoughts, the migration of your experiences, a ribbon of connection between your every breath. All your many moments, all your experiences, strung into one continuum—a single rushing current—as individual crystal beads might form a necklace. This is your river."

Eloquently, she continued. "The river speaks through you, Agnes. It asks you, 'What is important? What do you value more than anything else? What is the best thing in life?' You are asked to choose what to dive into with the whole of your fevered heart! Listen. Listen closely, little one, and you will always hear its mellifluous whisper, for these creative waters are without end. They flow, flow, flow without limit.

"Like all gifts, this river is best shared. Share your wonder. Share your life. Perhaps you enjoyed the flavour I offered you?" The goddess nodded toward the tiny cups they had each emptied. "You drank from my river of moonlight. You drank my joy. When you pour a cup of your own essence for others to taste, its flavour—uniquely yours—can be fully savoured only when you drink it with friends. Sharing intensifies its character. Share the stream of your gifts to ensure that your river continuously flows, flows, flows freely, and to develop the fullness of its tone and resonance. Do this, and you will find your own experience intensifies as well."

She stood serene then, offering her own haiku:

"As the dragonfly
plaiting wild love in the wind.
Inspiration's song.

"Sit for a while with Hamsa, and he will share a further gift," Sarasvati invited, then wishing the pilgrims farewell, her splendour flooded the forest with light as she took her leave.

The melody of her voice echoed. "Remember: the worlds you sing into being are real. Sing, my friends! Sing your heart's desire."

Hamsa's meditation
a practice

"In all things of nature, there is something of
the marvelous."

– ARISTOTLE

Laughing warmly, Hamsa asked, "Shall I teach you to fly?"

Agnes's eyes widened, and her brow lifted as she imagined
this possibility, before realizing that Hamsa's jocularity
masked a metaphor, not magic.

"Tenderly close your eyes," he instructed. "These movements are very subtle, so approach yourself with great kindness. Envision your chest as a bird's body. How gently would
you hold it? Receive the possibility that you can move more
fluidly. Breathe smoothly, becoming aware of the here and
now. Simply by attending to your breath's free passage from
outside your body, to inside your body, then back out again,
you create a continuous ribbon of breath.

"Don't try!" Hamsa insisted. "It's easier than that—much
easier. Give yourself over to gravity, your skin soft, your
bones pliant.

"Did you know that your heart has wings?" Hamsa probed.
"As you breathe, your lungs unfurl to expand your chest,
curling out toward the sides of your body, gracefully lifting

then releasing your ribs as mighty wings. They create movement and space—a sense of inner buoyancy.

"Become conscious of the area right behind your heart, then use your nose to inhale as if you could access that space. Inhale languidly, sweetly, filling the space behind your heart. Take your time . . . feel more than think."

The pilgrims enveloped themselves in their senses, surrendering to tender sensation.

"Imagine each breath that enters you widening out from that centre behind your heart," the small goose suggested. "When you're ready to exhale, breathe slowly as your breath leaves that space.

"Inhaling, feel your back ribs protract, widening like wings. Exhale . . . Inhale behind your heart, the skin on your back spreading open like the feathers of a powerful bird. With ease, your exhalation leaves you then, seeping out like a secret.

"Be gentle with your body's movements. Be gentle with your internal judgements. Be gentle. Gentle. Trust that you're doing it exactly right!

"Inhale and exhale as if you had all the time in the world, your abiding interest in the sensation of breathing all that you need for utter satisfaction.

"This is flying," the little goose whispered, his voice sounding like the wind and the clouds and the summer sun. "Each sweet inhalation, each sweet exhalation is your own migration. On the beating of your heart's wings, you soar through life. Enjoy the journey, this migration from there to here. From then to now. Suffuse yourself in the simple ease, the contentment, of this very here . . . this very now.

"Come back again and again to your breath. Give it the fullness of your attention. Don't try. Don't try," he repeated. "Do you feel it? You are flying!"

What was that ffffooom, ffffffooom, ffffffoom?

Agnes now understood. Flying wasn't a metaphor. Indeed, it was magic.

22

devotion

"We think that most important clues are large,
but the world loves to remind us
that they can be beautifully small."

- SUZANNE SIMARD

devotion

Agnes was utterly charmed by the design that G was creating. "Oooh, like stars!" She sat back on her heels, cupped her chin, and watched with great curiosity as he developed its pattern.

The two were hunkered low under the lush branches of an Ancient One, still jubilant to have discovered another of these incomparable old trees—twisted, gnarly, wide, and welcoming. Of course, the group had stopped to offer their respects. G had asked Streak and ChiChi to clear away the leaves on the tree's east side. Retrieving fragrant blossoms from the forest had been entrusted to Finder. With a handful of rice flour that he pulled from the saddlebag on his lion mount, G had then bent and begun to draw on the cleared ground.

Adroitly sifting the powder between his fingers, he used it to create a diagram of surprising intricacy. "It's called a *kolam*, Agnes—a painted prayer. My mother, Uma, taught me. First, we make a dot, just like those on ChiChi's fur." Ganapati's gentle eyes twinkled. "This forms a central source point. Like a seed, it's a place of germination that can expand outward as a seed would grow. From condensed possibility, intention ripples out to affect everything that surrounds it—as anything done with purpose always does. Then we add more dots, more potency. A collection of alternatives."

G continued to drizzle the powder onto the ground until an ashen grid of dots spread wide at his feet. "Now, we relate our dots, drawing lines between them."

"Like Streak's stripes?" Agnes asked.

"Exactly! These establish connections, in much the same way as our two feline travelling companions have developed their friendship," G elucidated. "Relationships appear between the dots, around the dots, just as the patterns of constellations derive from individual stars. They remind us that, while each of us is as distinct as a single light in the night sky, we are never isolated. Our associations and affiliations, these interconnections—with family, friends, books, songs, even foods—build a structure, a culture. Relationships form the architecture of our lives. Joys multiply when we collaborate, and sorrow is ameliorated. Our relationships then create an exchange of energy—a great ocean of fuel from which we make choices, draw memories, create, and then create again."

G was straightforward. "We focus. Beginnings. Growth. Connections. Our drawing reflects all the matters most dear to us—all that we value. With our diagram, we bring awareness to our thoughts and give them shape."

Captivated by the diagram's sinuous weave, and always ready to sink her hands into the cookie dough or into the garden soil, Agnes asked, "Can I help?"

G complied, shaking a mound of white powder into her palm.

"Like this!" he demonstrated, as they marked a space on the cleared ground between the roots of the Elder.

"We are writing this as an invitation to our friend Shri," G explained, guiding his complex design with precision. Elaborating and embellishing, lines became vines that burst into blossom. Others, the entwined bodies of ever-wriggling serpents. Shadow and light played their eternal game of contrast as the deep umbrage of earth juxtaposed the moon-white flour. Repetition and flow ferried their attentions—looping, lilting, curling—as the unbroken lines continuously wove around the diagram.

"If we compose a message like this upon our threshold, that place where we initiate our every morning, take our first steps into our every day, we ensure that Shri and her teachings accompany us wherever that day's journey takes us. Durga suggested we make a turn here, so this Ancient One marks a kind of threshold for our journey," G noted. "We aim to live a beautiful life, so we create beauty as our message. Inviting Shri into our thoughts, into our homes, and into our lives encourages her. Do you understand, Agnes? We bring Shri to mind so that we are always in the fine company of this glorious goddess."

Agnes nodded, longing to witness Shri's roseate splendour once again. Hopeful of that Auspicious One's imminent presence, Agnes wondered aloud, "Will she come then, G, once our invitation is made?"

Stepping back from the diagram, G tilted his large head quizzically. "Is she not here with us now, little one?" It was the girl's turn to tilt her head in confusion.

G clarified. "Consider this, Agnes: as an artist does, we've created form from our attention. Dancer, potter, poet, painter—it matters not. Pouring our concerns into expression, we communicate. Attention becomes form. This is art! We are telling ourselves a story—a story of meaning, a story of awareness—to savour this very moment more acutely. To love our lives! To value the sensations that we are experiencing. Evoking our innermost aspirations, illustrating them with our art, our hearts are imprinted with our desire for Shri's visitation. We show her that we treasure everything she represents. Shri will always arrive when our thoughts welcome her—she will come and she will stay," he insisted. "Quite simply, she cannot resist beauty." At this, G smiled, radiating contentment.

"It's a shame you've made your art here, though, G," Agnes voiced a gentle concern. "It's so wondrous, and yet look! Ants are already carrying off the flour." Indeed, on the drawing's periphery, a tiny army mustered. Agnes shooed at the creatures.

"Oh! Don't worry, Agnes," G reassured. "The *kolam* is meant for them as well. Do you know Rahu—the dark unknowing?" Agnes shook her head.

"Unknowing introduces fear," G explained. "The ants are Rahu's messengers, for fear never travels alone! Once we open the door to fear, it quickly multiplies, crawling at us from every side. From an itch of confusion clouding our decisions all the way to full-on debilitation, if we let fear in, it can be extremely difficult to control. So, instead, we feed it at the threshold, making an offering to Rahu's miniature emissaries. Do you remember what our friend Durga counselled about demons?"

Agnes did indeed! "She said we must face them, know them, and understand them. Is fear a demon?"

G smiled. "When unwelcome, it certainly can be! Fear is real, and we can't eradicate it. Of course, we wouldn't want to. Fear, as all emotions, has its place—there are moments when fear is *exactly* the right response! However, when it's unwanted, fear can take precedence. If we invite fear as a part of our experience, feed it with our interest, we can keep it at the doorway of our hearts and minds. But we don't invite it inside; we don't allow it to dominate us! Feeding the ants at the periphery reminds us of this hard-won lesson."

Bending back over their drawing, the two friends completed their offering to the Goddess Who Makes More. "I love these diagrams too," G admitted. "Of course, I love that they decorate doorways—after all, the threshold is my favourite place in the *whole* world!"

At this revelation, in spite of herself (for she really did know better), Agnes giggled. Of course, we all have our crazy predilections, but really?!

"Your favourite place is the THRESHOLD?!" Agnes fairly squealed, a bit embarrassed at her inability to better mask her surprise. "Ummm, dear Ganapati . . . please . . . you must tell me why."

Perhaps he was giving this little Canadian girl too much credit, G considered. Hesitating to point out the obvious (and most kindly stopping short of adding "duh!") he explained with gentle urgency. "Because it's the middle, Agnes. The in-between. We're always in the middle of the story. Even the edges are the middle of something!" As odd as she thought his love of the threshold, he found her lack of it just as strange. Who in heaven's name wouldn't love the threshold, this precious marker of possibility? Why . . . When one steps over a threshold, the doors to the whole universe open wide. And on the other side, opportunity awaits!

G attempted to state it as simply as he knew how. "It is the threshold that initiates any journey, Agnes." Surely, once he broke it down for her, she'd get it. "It is the bridge to beginning, a symbol of change. Not only does it mark the shift from here to there, it also excites with uncertainty."

"Like finally entering the gateway of the Lost Temple?" she asked.

G abruptly challenged this simplistic interpretation. "But was that the beginning, Agnes? Or did the adventure start when we first bumped off the slide? Or perhaps when you found the lighted balloon?"

Ohhhh . . . Yes!

Relief swelled in the Great Being as understanding beamed back from Agnes's eyes. "You mean, the great gates are simply 'A' beginning, G? HOLY SMOKE! I think I get it! You mean there's always a beginning before the beginning? And there's always an end after the end?"

"Yes!" A delighted G swelled in pride at her comprehension. "You've got it, Agnes! We were once there. Suddenly, we're here. Once it was then. And now . . . well, it's now!" He laughed. This really was a most cherished topic, and G's immense belly jiggled at this delectable discussion.

"The threshold is not one thing. Neither is it two. It is betweenness. An interval. A seam. And yet at the same time, it illustrates the continuity—as with the constellations we spoke of earlier. Between the stars, there exists a vast expanse of space, yet we link them. And from those connections, we create pictures and patterns and stories. With our art, we widen our options to accumulate perspective, and opening that liminal space, transform any journey into the Long Way Home. We take our time. We look around, admiring the scenery. We savour an experience more prolonged, more eventful—replete with the unanticipated."

G shivered expectantly. "We are not only open to surprises—we embrace them! This Long Way is when the getting there is more important than the destination. And sooooo . . . that means . . . as we step over the threshold . . . ANYTHING can happen!"

Agnes grinned. "Well, when you put it like that, G, I guess the threshold is one of my favourite places too!"

G's meditation
a practice

"Art is the tree of life."

– WILLIAM BLAKE

The group bowed their heads to the magnanimous Ancient One, as Streak laid a hibiscus as red as a flame atop the delicate rice-flour diagram that G and Agnes had completed. The others followed, each with their own offering. Ganapati then took a seat at the base of the Elder One's glorious, twisted trunk, and settling his own twisted trunk, closed his eyes and asked the others to join him.

"Like me, become familiar with the density of your bones," G suggested. "Can you fully succumb to the solidity of the ground beneath you? Earth, like a buoyant hammock, cradles you. Reach her with your fingertips. Touch her." Stretching their curiosity to the firmness under them, paws and hooves and tiny fingers recognized the earth.

"Your heaviness belongs to her," Ganapati continued. "It is of her that you are made."

Agnes eased her body into the ground, allowing herself to feel as heavy as G. As she did, a prolonged exhalation escaped, and she wondered how long it had been since she'd breathed this fully. She took another deep breath and savoured the release of letting it go.

227

"Do you feel yourself right here? Hands warm? Feet warm?" G asked. One by one, they nodded. Agnes felt the weight of her body, the heat of her blood. She heard her breath rise and fall, her heart's soft thrum, and felt the reassuring support of the earth. A deep appreciation of the long path they had journeyed welled up.

"Listen," Ganapati whispered to them. "Wait . . ." Agnes felt her ease translate to her eyes, felt her vision widen peripherally under her gently closed lids, sweet and curious.

Ganapati became a sound inside her. "Follow the sensations."

On the leisurely breeze, abundant flowers shared their scent. Agnes tasted the generosity of the forest in the sweetness of fresh fruits. She recalled the kind aid they had received from so many, the joy of companionship. Appreciation became sound. Sound became scent. Scent turned to feeling, to taste, to gratitude. Emotions and flavours melded and merged. Colours shifted into textures, light translated to warmth, then to a brightness in her heart.

"Follow the sensations." G's hush repeated like an enchantment.

A breeze ruffled, and grass brushed her bare shins. A distant crow.

The sound of G's breath . . . ChiChi's . . . then Streak's . . . Each friend's rhythm met her own with a tender connection. Nothing between her breath and the murmur of the Ancient One's leaves. Near and far coalesced.

She slipped down, down, down into unfocused awareness.

Ganapati, regal on a throne of multicoloured gems—a prismatic array of flickering ruby, emerald, citrine, and turquoise. Light refracted/pulsed/shimmered. Hearts unfurled like seashells. Stretched wide like open wings. Enraptured, each friend filled her sky.

Mountain ranges of kindness.

Rivers of ideas.

Oceans of dreams.

Internally, her breath called to her . . . called to her . . . called to her . . . until lightly, lightly, she was back . . . back under her eyelids, back under the Elder . . . back with the outflowing warmth of all her wonderful, wondrous friends.

She sighed, and her eyes opened . . . and looked to G.

"You have travelled with me to visit the three worlds of my mother," Ganapati explained. "While awake, we live only in this world, see only with our eyes. With Earth's aid, we burrow into the realms of the other worlds within us, welcoming our blind spots, our shadows, all the hidden unexplored corners of ourselves. Within her abiding affirmation, our perspective widens to encompass the vast multiplicity of being--its complexities, its entanglements, its plenitude and relationships. As we allow life to flow through us—through all of us—we experience synesthesia. And when our senses interact in this way, we can excavate fantastic treasures. This is how we recover not only our own recollections but also the memories of the ancestors. This is how we remember."

"Dearest Ganapati," Agnes's words tumbled out with excitement, "I did remember! I remembered the sparkle of the

River Goddess on water! I remembered why she seemed familiar! The map! The map that fell from the stars! The map is the goddess—or the goddess is the map! Friends, do you see?!"

At this revelation, at this deep remembrance, the companions bolted to their feet. Agnes dug into voluminous pockets to retrieve the curl of yellowed paper that the lighted balloon had delivered over a fortnight ago. She spread open its tight twist. With renewed wonder at the pattern it revealed, the pilgrims stared down at the wrinkled map, ready now for this night's adventures.

The Lost Temple's inner secrets felt very, very close . . .

23

perspective

"Vismayoyogabhumikah"
(The worlds of deep engagement are astonishing.)

– SHIVA SUTRAS

perspective

Tracing the lines and angles of the etchings on the map with her small finger, Agnes exclaimed, "This! This is the diagram of the sparkles on the water. The River Goddess was relaying a message about the map! Why didn't I see it before? It was right here!" (Once inspiration comes, doesn't it always seem so obvious?)

The others leaned in close, jostling for a better view. Furry brows lifted, eyes widened, and breath of all varieties sucked powerfully inward. Even the busy lives of the forest seemed to hesitate.

Finder finally asked the very question on everyone's lips: "But . . . what IS the message?"

Streak shook his head heavily, and if cheetahs have shoulders, ChiChi shrugged his. Frustration tightened the little girl's chest. They could all recognize the pattern. They understood that the River Goddess had reiterated its value—but what was its meaning? That proved elusive still.

"Durga directed us to turn east here." Ganapati offered a plan to counter their deflation. "Let's stick with it and keep going!"

And so they did, bushwhacking through thickets and brambles for hours and hours until—exhausted from their efforts and with dawn nearing—they chose a small glade in which to rest. Nestling against the broad side of the giraffe, the little girl plucked burrs and thistles from ChiChi's fur. Streak explored, and Ganapati dozed, his elephant head propped on his lion mount, big belly rippling with each soft snore.

His energy still high, Streak sniffed and snuffled, poked and padded around the perimeter of the open meadow of their camp. Sensing something special, he bounded back to the group. "Look what I've come upon!" he purrrrred, his pleasure at this discovery wholly evident.

Startled from his nap, G and the others rose to follow. And sure enough, at the far edge of the clearing, everyone witnessed an odd gleam emanating from within the forest. Crowding closer, they inspected a stone column, its pallor gently luminous against the darkened alcove within which it stood. A smooth stone, it was not much taller than Agnes, but upon seeing it, G immediately dropped to his knees, and bowing his torso low, touched his brow to the earth.

"It's called a *lingam,*" he stated simply as he stood, then slipped back to the meadow. Returning with a handful of wildflowers, Ganapati scattered the bright petals over the pillar, explaining further. "This is my father—my father in his Formless Form."

With hands over their hearts, each member honoured the great Shining One, Shiva. "He's very beautiful," Agnes whispered, moved by the pillar's stately elegance.

"Yes," Ganapati replied.

"And very, very powerful," Finder added, noting the aura that radiated from the stone.

To that, G nodded, repeating, "Yes."

"Do you think he is here to help us?" ChiChi asked hopefully.

Again, Ganapati nodded. "Of that, there is no doubt!" Optimism illuminated everyone's eyes before G curbed their rising spirits. "Since he chose to assume this particular appearance, however, he's not going to make it easy!"

All eyes remained fixed on the strength of this glowing monolith at the edge of the forest. Sunlight filtered through the leaves, speckling the forest floor with mysterious shapes. G sighed. "Dad loves a good puzzle."

Unexpectedly, Agnes clapped. "A game? But G, you know I LOVE puzzles!"

"Well, you might not like his," G cautioned. "Dad tends to cheat—and you'll find his answers always elicit more questions."

At this Agnes laughed. "G!" she chided. "Remember? You told me the exact same thing! The best answer is always to pose a better question—that's just what you said." G chuckled happily. The little girl had been listening, and that was good.

Ever so slowly, the group circled the Formless Form. Moving clockwise, they contemplated. They ruminated. They chewed on bottom lips, furrowed brows, squinted . . . Fingers tapped. Toes tapped. What? What? What? Settling on the ground around the towering stone, they speculated and meditated and conferred. Just what riddle might the Lord of the Three Realms be posing?

Finally in utter befuddlement (and perhaps a bit bored with this quandary), they began to tell stories.

The giraffe shared the fruits he'd picked, then stretched a befittingly tall tale which had them all rolling on the ground in mirth, chewed lips and tapping digits forgotten. Each in turn entertained the others, until together, they told themselves their own story—the story of this journey they'd undertaken. They recounted how they'd met; convulsed into hysterics at their many missteps; and delighted themselves with the narration of adventures, of bravery, of shared successes. Brilliance sparked, as together they stitched their five vantage points into one memory. From giraffe heights to little-girl lows, from the night vision of cats and the olfactory glory of elephants. The story became more, became full and fat and whole, as the companions seamlessly wove their distinct perspectives into a single exuberant, deliciously boisterous tale. A true quest. A journey of discovery. Of the meaning of friendship. Of exploring the depth of capabilities. Of reflection, and yes, of magic. The magic of insight. The magic of growth. The alchemy of the Long Way Home.

When they finished, each became quiet, replete in the others' fine company. They were content. One by one, hands and paws and hooves met and held fast.

"WaitwaitwaitwaitwaitwaitwaitwaitwaitwaitWAAAAAIT!!!"

Startled from the silence of their contemplations, they all looked to Agnes, squawking like a ravenous fledgling. "I think I might have something!" Small hands dove back into deep pockets. Out came a bit of string—no, not that. Out came a tiny bone—no, not that. Sidelong eyes shifted to sidelong eyes. Some impatient squirming ensued. Out came a bag of crumpled crisps—Ooooh! She passed them to the giraffe, who divvied them up, and patience returned as they nibbled thoughtfully.

"Aha! Yup! Got it!" Agnes muttered, revealing the yellowed map once again. Waving it triumphantly, she then flattened it out on the ground. All eyes converged.

"Okay . . ." She began to trace the lines again, hesitating at a corner. "Remember the first of the Ancient Ones? The illustrious Tree of the World?" The pilgrims' heads nodded in unison. As disparate pieces began to form interlocking connections, Agnes's thoughts tumbled out faster and faster, with little space between. Sentences gushed forth at a breakneck rhythm, with the companions hard-pressed to follow. "Wasn't this where the path suddenly forked? The one we chose first was a dead end—remember? We had to turn back? Back to where we'd started? Then we took the other fork . . ."

Crumpled foreheads attempted to pursue her wordy jumble.

Fumbling back into her pocket, she pulled out a handful of her gathered mementos. "First we found The Tree of the World." Dramatically, she dropped a green pebble at the bend in the diagram's perimeter. "And that's where we turned and started up that steep hill!"

Eyebrows lifted. Losing no momentum at this fizzle of a response, Agnes continued her nonstop verbal torrent.

"Look, we forged the river here." Her finger slid farther along the stained paper, tracing the hint of another line. "Walked the far bank! Passed through the valley! Then that thick forest, before we scaled that huge mountain—remember? Remember?! All that fog? All that rain?"

Flamboyantly, like a chess piece, a whorled seashell landed on the map. "Then we found another Elder Tree and *that's* when we turned to climb again!" Giraffe and cat heads began nodding, as understanding swept through the group. Indulgently, Ganapati smiled. (I told you that what he didn't know wasn't worth knowing!)

"And here! That cliff? The path that hugged the steep canyon? The cloud forest—the snowy owl's warning—the everlasting moraine—that other giant mountain?!!" Dramatic pause. "That's when Durga told us to travel east to visit one of the Most Ancients!" And at the wide wonder of this revelation, she placed a tiny pinecone emphatically on the map. "We turned again and up, up, up we went!" Throwing open her arms then, the verbal barrage ended. Agnes sat back on her heels, looking expectantly from face to face.

Concise as ever, ChiChi sought consolidation. "So, our circuitous route created a spiral, the Ancient Ones mark a turning point, the map is really in 3D, and we've been ascending all along?"

"Exactly, ChiChi!" Excitement brightened each face. "We're not only on the right path but we must be almost there! Now that we understand how the map works, I think we can get to the inner sanctum of the Lost Temple tonight!"

"Fan-xxx-tas-xxx-tic!" Finder's speech was garbled as he transitioned once more to silver simian, then offered his fresh reconnaissance. "I will climb to the canopy and report back!" Whooping, he wheeled off into the trees, as Streak and ChiChi efficiently broke camp.

Tipping his trunk toward the Formless Form, G quizzed Agnes: "So, Dad wasn't helpful after all then?"

Adamantly, Agnes countered. "Quite the contrary, dear Ganapati! My epiphany came about as a sun-shaft crept across your father. The light assumed different qualities, evoked different feelings, as luminosity and shadows interacted, creating a distinctive vision."

She bit her lip, struggling to explain the inspiration. "With each movement, G, different possibilities emerged. Your father's height became more obvious; then his fullness caught my eye. In the shimmer of light, there was activity. Faces and figures shaped from his formlessness. All of a sudden, I realized that not for one fraction of a second was he ever actually still! Do you see, G?" Her chin tilted as she met the kind eyes of the Great Being. "The Formless Form isn't one thing but many—just like the story of our adventure isn't just one story but all our stories. Oneness shows itself in plurality—that's what makes it great! Your father's very formlessness disguises his diversity. I got it, G. I just got it. Anything is possible! It just depends on opening yourself up to the big picture!"

Jubilant (and rather proud) that Agnes had broken the code and received his father's teaching, G turned back to the mighty stone pillar as the others left the clearing. Lifting his left leg to mimic his father's most beloved dance—one arm curled to veil his heart, another open-palmed—he twisted his trunk toward the ripe mango he had been saving until later. *Life is sweet,* he danced to his father. Low on the horizon, the sun filtered through the leaves at the clearing's edge, dappling the Formless Form in a glow like lambent flames. The pillar rotated, rotated again, spinning, spinning, spinning wildly, morphing the resplendent *lingam* into the Dancing Lord Nataraja. For a single moment—or was it an eternity? —father and son danced together in the shadow and light of the great Forest of Consciousness.

Then—with a deep bow and broad wink—Ganapati climbed onto Simha's back and, crossing the threshold of the forest to the path, travelled on to join his friends.

full moon

24

the eternals

"From moonlit place to place,
the sacred moon overhead has taken a new phase."

- W. B. YEATS

the eternals

A path so narrow that breath nearly stilled. Nightfall now, so early. What luck that a full moon rose to brindle the forest floor with its diffuse light!

Slow going . . .

Treacherous . . .

Each step required great care, with an awareness as full as the effulgent moon . . .

The grounds of the inner temple were expansive, yet tangled with vines and piercing brambles. Creepers caught their limbs, tethering their feet to the ground—like lonely souls anxious for visitors, reluctant to release them. Alleys opened into shadows like gaping maws, and squawking from their black obscurity, howlers settled to sleep. Minuscule bats traced elegant arabesques—odes to the moonlight. Atop the temple's crumbling walls, smoky silhouettes of strange figures rose up, coalesced into form, then dissipated once again. Were they real or imagined?

Each companion carried the length and complexity of this splendid journey in their every cautious move. Was the goal finally at hand?

Fear clotted in the little girl's throat. Looking up at the moon, pale and serene, Agnes admired how she had accompanied them throughout their entire pilgrimage. Whether as a sliver of silver or as this now lustrous orb, the moon had always been there—even when she'd hidden in her own darkness. She shared aspects of herself, yet was eternally present as herself—always full, even when appearing as pieces. And each phase of her light, while distinct, was equally glorious, each distinction a hint of her true capacity.

Recalling how Durga had explained that the intelligence behind terror ensured that one was totally present and aware, Agnes considered how she might imitate the moon, accepting this fear she felt as simply one phase of her own experience. *"Fear brings you fully to the party,"* the great goddess had counselled. So, as Durga taught, Agnes softened her skin to receive the fear until her breath returned to its natural fluidity. Her focused gaze then shifted between the glowing sky and the knotted brambles, between the vast celestial expanse and the need for vigilance. Enveloped by infinite light fragments, the world around her—bespeckled with moonlight—mirrored the starry heavens. Stippling prisms dappled her clothes, transforming Agnes into another piece of the night.

She realized that she belonged.

Wrapped in this cloak of concealment, assimilated into the night, her curiosity surged. The darkness held such promise of discovery. She found herself delighting in the mystery—the anticipation of the unexpected. Cool air tingled her lips, awakening her lungs. Silently, she sighed it back out, and like a tonic, each new breath brightened her spirit. Was her vision sharper? Her hearing? She thought so. Smiling at her secret, she savoured another inhalation, another exhalation, ease honing her senses.

The moon travelled the sky. The stars shifted. A long breeze quivered leaves and branches. Each subtle transition cast the variegated light into action, and the universe whorled about Agnes. Buoyed on its serpentine wave, Agnes took her every step in alignment with the stars. Like a message, the night spoke to her as she expanded herself into its current. Overwhelmed by the pleasure of partnership—with her friends, with the trees, with the path under her feet, with the sky and the wind and the movement of the moonlight. All her attention was here. Only here.

In complete participation, her consciousness no longer just her own, Agnes widened into imagination's full field. She understood the calls of the night creatures, the voice of the wind. She inhaled the scent of the stars, heard the moonlight, felt the owl's screech on the hairs of her arms. Agnes ceased to be just herself. The seams of time and space and being disappeared. As expansive as the sky, Agnes was now herself and everything else too. A helix of swirling light. A snake's silken skin. Leaves that fluttered tirelessly, shivering with a love of life, of growth, of green goodness . . .

Capturing sound with G's acuteness, seeking movement in the shadows with the cats' keen night vision, and from a towering height, as the giraffe, she sought out a clear path. As if familiar with this place, Agnes understood the way. Slithering the asking path, her vision undulated, curved, and twisted around the obstacles. Each exhalation issued forth as the wind from an endless source within her, and she sparkled with the prismatic fantasies of the moon to light the trail.

Uma's meditation
a practice

"Live in the sunshine, swim the sea, drink the wild air."
-RALPH WALDO EMERSON

As the pilgrims approached the heart of the Temple, its essence became a palpable and powerful presence. Hearts raced.

Recognizing this mounting anxiousness, G leaned into his own skills to help everyone remain grounded: "Please relax and listen, friends. I will share a teaching of my mother's."

Warmly he teased, "After all, it won't help much if we find the Temple's centre but lose our own." All acknowledged this wisdom, and turned to face their sagacious G.

"'Umaa . . .'" Ganapati began. "Shiva murmurs the name of his eternal beloved, my mother, the beneficent goddess Uma. She is prana—life personified as breath—and their lovemaking forms the very dance of creation.

"When we're born," G explained, "breath is given to us. We're under no obligation to do anything more. We breathe with or without attention, our bodies vehicles for this collaboration of the life force both inside and outside of ourselves. Indeed, we could go our whole lives without further consideration of this energy and still this generous goddess would breathe us—offering her own radiance so that we too might shine.

"What might it mean," G challenged his friends, "to conceive of breath as a divinity, as a goddess? What does it convey to assign a value so refined—the value of sacredness—to this pre-eminent aspect of our lives? For in every gentle inhalation, in every soft exhalation, is our breath not life itself?

"Like Shiva's tender moan to his True Love, our breath maintains a conversation," G continued. "We breathe in the universe, and as we exhale, we release some of our own vitality in an interchange with the world around us.

"This meditation asks what happens if we turn the currency of our attention to our breath. It asks what happens when we inhale and exhale like deities making love. Pillowing awareness on our breath, we ask the goddess, 'Would you like to dance?' And . . . we *always* let her lead!" he empha-sized, laughing.

"Consciously admire Uma's gift of breath. Savour the nuances, the grace with which it enters our bodies. This is a very simple practice. Step back from any need to direct or manage," he suggested. "Instead, just allow breath to pass, creating an accommodating conduit for vitality.

"Remember, dear ones: each time we meditate, we start over. Fresh. New. Just this breath. Just this moment." G's reminders were gentle but firm. "Let us ask no more of our-selves than to experience what we experience. To relish it!

"Aim to enter this reflection in supreme comfort." Ganapati himself rested against his mount, Simha. "Sit in ease. Build your environment like a bird assembling a nest." At this instruction, Agnes laid Apasmara's woolly shawl across her legs, and ChiChi and Streak curled closer, encircling the giraffe.

"We keep our gaze unfocused, and we drop our awareness onto our breath. Let our soft eyes initiate their own closure, each breath sweet. Each breath easy. No rush. No hurry. Patiently, we wait to inhale. We let it happen. We wait again. Our exhalation leaves us—all without pushing, without pulling. When we slow down to accord our breath its own time, the next inhalation and the next exhalation will both take longer than we expect. Keep in mind, we have time. Lots of time," G reassured them.

"Begin to count, inhaling for four, three, two, one . . . Exhale for four, three, two, one . . . Each count takes about a second. Go through a few rounds of breath just like this."

Agnes nodded, and slowing down, allowed her breath to initiate movement. Slowly. Steadily. It was heavenly, and she savoured it.

"When you're ready, add one count. Inhale for five, four, three, two one . . . Exhale for five, four, three, two, one . . . Inhale for five, four, three, two, one . . . Exhale for five, four, three, two, one . . ."

"Can you sense the delicate pause between inhaling and exhaling? Between exhalation and the next inhalation?" G asked. "We are not holding our breath. The pause might be only a second. Just take note of it. Sense it. It's a suspension of action. Don't try to hold it! Longer is not a goal. Only ease. Only effortlessness. Let yourself be breathed. Our breath carries its own innate intelligence; there is no need for us to do anything more.

"Inhale: five, four, three, two, one. Hesitate . . . Then exhale: five, four, three, two, one, hesitate again . . . Five, four, three, two, one, hesitate . . . Five, four, three, two, one, hesitate.

"Between each breath, a suspended moment—like time swinging in a hammock. The pendulum ebbs, then returns on its own. Ebbs and returns. Ebbs and returns . . .

"The rhythm of our breath remains unhurried. We don't struggle."

"Freely in, freely out. In . . . Out . . . In . . . Out . . . No rush."

"Once established, maintain that rhythm, but stop counting. Instead, we'll choose a place where we'd like to *feel* our breath. At the tip of our noses as a cool inhalation, a warm exhalation? Or perhaps the lift and fall of our bellies? Choose one place and focus on that sensation. Imagine life's vibrancy infusing us with each inhalation, as our exhalation floats us aloft as if on a wave."

"Five, four, three, two, one. Hesitate . . . Five, four, three, two, one. Hesitate . . ."

"Sustain that languid rhythm, as each breath calls the goddess's name. Umaa . . . Umaa . . . You are both Mother and Father, divinity in conversation.

"Hear yourself whisper to her . . .whisper your love…

"Umaa . . . Umaa . . ."

25
the inner temple

"No need for temples.
No need for complicated philosophy.
Your own mind, your own heart is the temple."

– TENZIN GYATSO, DALAI LAMA XIV

the inner temple

I n the vast columned halls of the inner sanctum, shadows deepened remarkably. Sound was muffled: only the odd bat echolocating; an erratic symphony of tiny frogs; the splash of dampness drip, drip, dripping on old stone. With vision compromised—the giraffe's soft glow was quickly swallowed, and even the great cats were struggling—the group could only feel their way.

Deeper, deeper . . .

Pleated into the darkness between the columns, decaying statuary stood a lost guard. Forgotten languages silenced the tale of the carved inscriptions underfoot. At long last, the travellers—these true friends—found themselves at the heart of the Lost Temple. Its central citadel loomed into the sky above them, an imposing stone turret with multiple levels and walls so sheer there was nothing to grasp, nothing with which they could ascend. As one, the group sighed.

However, the little Canadian girl was not to be denied.

"We're too close!" she whispered, and from her voluminous pockets, extracted a length of hemp cord. All watched as she scuttled up high on the column opposite the tower. Looping her rope, and tying it off . . . she leapt with a wild yelp (Of fear? Yes! Of elation? Yes!) and a triumphant whoosh, swinging across the courtyard towards the tower, arcing wide. All eyes—hers too—clenched tightly closed as she careened inelegantly, splatting hard against the tower wall, and sliding ever so slowly, ever so awkwardly, back to the courtyard's stone floor.

"Errooofff!" she groaned as her friends surrounded her.

Ganapati held out a hand, hoisting her up. "Why don't we just take the stairs?" he suggested, nodding deeper towards the interior. Agnes rolled her eyes. *Really?!*

In a flash, the embarrassing episode was forgotten, as they nimbly sprinted up the precipitous steps. Chunks of stone crumbled here and there. Ever more arduous as they neared the top, they slowed to avoid rubble and gaping cracks.

"Careful!" ChiChi warned the giraffe. "The ceiling dips here." They had reached the peak.

Silence.

"What does it mean?" Agnes asked no one—and everyone.

Silence.

For at the very, very top, at the pinnacle of this command-ing structure, at the end of this sustained journey, this epic journey, this journey of days and weeks, of adventures bold and with periods of lassitude, of inclement weather, and perilous territory, of fast friendships and expanded hearts, of an infinitude of immense kindnesses, of strangers and stranger beings, of demons and celestials, at this very, very peak . . . someone was already there.

For a candle burned low, its wee light illuminating a vermil-lion mark at the centre of the floor. Was it blood? Agnes bent low to examine it. Yet another clue? She hunkered down, leaning in closer . . . closer . . . Trying, trying to understand. A little closer. She cocked her head. Contorted her brow. Squinted. Closer . . . closer . . .

And.

Then.

She.

Fell.

Right.

In.

An illusion—that's what it was. That red daub on the floor was an actual opening—a keyhole? A passageway?

Call it what you will, but through this portal she fell. Twisting and tumbling. Tumbling and twisting. Flower petals fluttered wildly through the air around her like so many butterflies. Orange and yellow and pink. There was sweet smoke too. Bells clamoured, jangling their mighty ruckus. Horns bleated and whined. Drums beat, beat, beat . . . while down and down and down she fell, through this colossal hullabaloo.

Anticipating the bottom, she tensed . . .

26
home

"The journey itself is my home."

- BASHO

home

And rolled onto her back . . . Lifting her head, shielding her eyes *(so bright!)*, she swept back a mussed curtain of hair, and peeped through squeezed lids. *Where am I? Is this . . . my bedroom?* Sunshine glinted and glimmered off fresh snow, flooding her room with winter-white light. Out the window, the postman zigzagged down the block, arms stacked high with letters and packages as he picked his way through snowy mounds.

Agnes shook her head, trying to comprehend. What had just happened? Had it all been a dream? How disappointing! Simply a dream? Was that possible?

"Hhhhhmph!"

ChiChi . . . Streak . . . the transforming Finder . . . GANAPATI! Her heart sank as the little Canadian girl realized that her big adventure—this splendid journey full of magical beings—had simply been a single night's restless sleep.

She felt the tight grip of her clenched hand. Freeing her small fingers, she looked down. Now her eyes opened fully! Incredulous at the oddity of it, she gazed at a diminutive, mottled seed . . . cupped in her palm like an egg in its nest. Holy smoke! How the heck did that get there?!

"Hhhhhmph!" she repeated, and sliding open her bedside drawer, placed the seed inside her box of Very Special Things. She reached for Big Eye and peered down. Yup, it was a seed all right. A tiny, speckled seed. *How curious!*

Slipping her feet into fuzzy pink slippers, rather disconsolate, she flounced down the hallway, and perched on a stool in the kitchen. When one believes one has had a miraculous journey of discovery, then finds it was nothing but a dream . . . Well, who wouldn't feel a bit cheated?

On the counter, a bowl of cereal sat ready for her.

Her gratitude was rather rote given her current crestfallen state. "Thanks, Momma."

"You're welcome, dear!" Momma sang back. "By the way, the mailman left you a letter. It's right there beside your cereal."

"Whaddya mean? A letter for me?!"

"Agnes!" her mother chastised from the other room. "Please enunciate!"

She might have corrected herself, her eyes might have rolled, or perhaps her shoulders might have shrugged, but at the sight of the elephant stamp on the envelope, Momma's gentle correction was completely forgotten. Agnes's ears rang with a mighty ruckus, and she dropped her spoon with a piercing jangle as her heart beat-beat-beat!

It was thin, the envelope. Blue, and as pale as a winter sky. Brushing aside the petals—orange and yellow and pink— fallen from her mother's vase, Agnes tore open an edge and slid a note from inside.

On crisp vellum, in a delicate script, it read as follows:

27

the letter

"... the end and the beginning are always there,
before the beginning and after the end."

– T. S. ELIOT

Dear One,

Yesterday's mystery may be solved, but another mystery always follows. You think you have dreamed. Consider instead that you have just explored the Lost Temple inside yourself. Now, a new threshold awaits.

For each day is a door to be opened. Each breath, a gift you receive as an invitation to begin. As with any true gift, there is no reason, no purpose, no goal. Its meaning—and if it has meaning—is simply up to you.

No answers, only better questions.

Remain curious! Embrace all the possibilities between here and there, between now and then.

If you devote yourself fully, you will find the Lost Temple in every idea, in every project. As with our journey, realization comes little by little, as you step again and again, until you locate the Temple within.

It is up to you which idea you explore, which journey you take, which story you write into being, then share. For each is a seed. Each yields the unexpected.

So, why not write a grand tale? Why not have a great adventure?

Enter the conversation and remember: keep good company, always. There is no obstacle we can't overcome together.

Create a life you love, Agnes, and may you flourish in your joy!

> *Ever thine,*
>
> *G*

PS. Shri asked me to pass along her message: you are as infinite as the Universe—How could you be anything else?

28

the threshold

"There is a light that shines beyond all things on Earth, beyond us all—beyond the highest, the very highest heavens. This is the light that shines in our heart."

- CHANDOGYA UPANISHAD

the threshold

Agnes considered the tiny seed which rested now, snug in her treasure box. *Spring is just around the corner,* she thought, *the perfect time to begin a garden.* Meanwhile, with fresh snow just fallen, there were new friends to meet, old friends to enjoy, and a novel landscape to explore. Low spirits vanished as she hurriedly finished her breakfast, then dressed, zipping up her parka and pulling on a woolly toque.

"Going out to play, Momma!" she called.

At the door to this brilliant day, the little Canadian girl hesitated for a golden moment in the blinding brightness. Looking down to her feet, down at the threshold, she grinned broadly as she glimpsed her shadow dancing playfully on the other side. Her eyes closed, and she inhaled a slow breath. A very slow breath. She savoured it. And then another.

She let gravity hold her as she exhaled a haiku to Ganapati, to Sarasvati, to Shri—to all the Shining Lights who accompanied her always on her journey through this world:

> *This threshold moment,*
> *a promise realized—*
> *diligence, beauty.*

Eyes open again—open wide to the wide-open day—she took a bounding leap up, up, up and over the threshold . . . joining her shadow in the radiant light.

What magic awaited her under this sunny sky, where ANYTHING can happen?!

the end

(IS JUST A NEW BEGINNING)

You are the mystery you seek.

. . . aum . . .

cast of characters:
celestials + pilgrims

Symbolizing aspects of our human experience—universal energies, psychological constructs, unseen forces, and physical realities—the gods are *devatas*, the literal Shining Lights. They represent the sublime, the ethereal, the unconscious made visible, the aggregate that disrupts your expectations, the powers that collaborate with your dreams.

When we align with these energies, we find delight in effort and involvement, understand the necessities of relationship, and expose the value in passion; when we are with the gods, we draw all these systems into our conscious action. We bring the shadow of the unknown into the light of awareness.

The Hindu celestials are known as the 330 million—in other words, they are infinite in number, infinitely varied and infinitely complex. As to their meaning, there are as many interpretations as there are practitioners.

Agnes: The little Canadian Girl is everyone who ever went on a journey of discovery. Her name is a derivation of Agni, the Indian god of fire, one of the most important deities in the Rigveda—the world's oldest ritual text in continued use. In the smoke that comes from fire, Agni provides the communication between humanity and the celestials, as fire can transform anything from one thing to another. (Agnes's preferred exclamation, "Holy Smoke!" winks at this reference.)

When fire is used as a metaphor within our bodies, it represents the flames of ardour, the heat of willpower. Feeding our passions with desire and commitment, we accommodate our own immense potential for transformation. As one of the gateways to the *devatas,* Agni maintains the access from immediate experience to an experience of the collective unconscious.

Apasmara: Quite commonly demonized, Apasmara is the symbol of forgetting. As such, many call him "ignorance," yet Apasmara wields tools: his curving serpent represents unconscious anxieties snaking under the surface of our thoughts and actions, and his short, sharp dagger, our discernment. Rather than a simple binary of good/bad, he illustrates that forgetting carries more nuanced possibilities. And indeed, when most-famously depicted under Nataraja's dancing foot, Apasmara's continuum of forgetting and remembrance provides the foundational support for Shiva's eternal recursive movement from creation to maintenance to dissolution and back to creation again.

ChiChi, the cheetah: Described as an intoxication, Soma is the mythical elixir of the ancient Vedas, and what intoxicates us more fully than the joy we find in effort? All work done with full awareness returns to us an unrivalled inner gratification. ChiChi represents this energy.

Durga: The Indomitable Spirit, Durga is the radiant pool of wisdom arising from the ocean of consciousness; the river of prana's force flowing as an even breath; a body divinized through mindful care and a clear mind. She exemplifies the fire within—the fire that manifests as courage and determination. When profound integrity births righteous action, when indefatigable persistence results in a singular focus, we have embodied Durga. Her character suggests that a challenge met with full and sincere effort will always proffer success.

Finder, the giraffe/silver ape: Symbolic of transformation, this shapeshifter reminds us that we all possess abilities yet unrecognized (by ourselves, as well as by others), and no matter which of our hats we are currently wearing, we are still ourselves. We morph, yet we retain, layering our capacities in a complex network of growth and development, just as while a giraffe, Finder can never conceal the glowing silver of his ape fur.

G/Ganapati: Ganapati is perhaps the most beloved of Hinduism's 330 million celestials. One of his many epithets is the Lord of Thresholds: the quality of observing the potential for growth in a movement from here to there, this to that, now to then. Location, attitude and ability, time—change in any of these areas affects who we are, and Ganapati symbolizes this energy of transition. Described as both the Obstacle as well as the Remover of Obstacles, Ganapati is a boundary, something we come up against and must find a way through or around. How to do that? Often, it is by simply recognizing the vital fact that the difficulties in our way illustrate the very route through those hindrances—that we manifest our own challenges as well as their solutions. Depicted as a boy with an elephant head, Ganapati exudes stability and responsibility—as befits his elephantine presence. When we feel grounded, when we feel at home in our skin, we are sourcing Ganapati energy.

"G" is a pun on Ji, the Indian term of endearment and respect. Finding ourselves acquainted with another's heart, we indicate this by calling them Ji, or adding Ji after their name.

The Green Mother: The Green Mother (*Paccai Amman*) is our own verdant planet, the Earth as the womb of all life. We are born on her, of her, and live our lives through the opulence of her blessings. Without Earth, we would not be.

Not simply a location, Earth manifests the processes of evolution, revealing the memory of all who have enjoyed a life on this planet. How many moons have waxed and waned in her billions of years of existence? How many waves have crashed her innumerable shores? As a loving mother, Earth remembers each subtle movement, each profound change of her progeny, then exhibits those transformations in her own irrepressible growth. She is the residue of summer lightening strikes, the spore on the curl of a fern frond, the avalanche on the lone mountain peak, and the crush of the city's madding crowds. In the splatter of rain and the silent upthrust of a mushroom, in raven's caw and cobra's hiss—indeed, in every utterance of every voice in every language, she tells and retells her countless tales.

As the utterly bewitching as well as the utterly quotidian, Earth illustrates the influence and persistence of memory: initiating life, then surrounding, permeating, and supporting it. Contingent upon those collected memories that shape her, our lives articulate this echo of the past. In this story, those memories are given form by Morning's Glory, movement through the Holder of String (the spider, Bhu), and expansion as the twisted branching network of the Ancient Ones, the revered elder trees of the Forest of Consciousness that germinate within the Earth, grow from the Earth, then return their roots to the Earth. As we all do.

Hamsa: An unassuming little goose (the Barred Himalayan Goose) that migrates tremendous distances at near-unimaginable heights—soaring over the highest mountains on earth—Hamsa symbolizes the greatest force held in the most unexpected vessel. He is the familiar or vehicle of Sarasvati and represents our breath, an energy whose power is also masked by its ubiquity and ordinariness. His wings are our lungs, and his very name, an onomatopoetic representation of the sound of our inhalation and exhalation.

Hanuman: The son of Wind, Hanuman symbolizes the vitality of passion and emotion. In the stories of India, his famed leaps are many—born of curiosity, of kindness, of the depths of loyalty, and of remarkable courage.

The Journey: Is the quest itself a character? Journey is the literal translation of the *yajña*, the sacred fire. It symbolizes the search we must make when considering the meaning and value of our lives. At the *yajña*, the fire god Agni acts as mediator, ferrying our communications in his smoke to the great forces of the cosmos—the celestial Shining Lights. As fire's heat transmutes the offerings made to it, so our own inner fire—willpower informed by focused awareness—transforms our lives. This journey of transformation, of reflection and the action that reflection initiates, is poignantly conveyed in the term the Long Way Home, where it is the pilgrimage itself that holds the teaching—never the destination.

Krishna: The essence of abiding love, Krishna's dark presence lives in the beauty of the midnight sky, allowing the luminosity of the stars to shine with more brilliance—just as the love of our family and friends encourages the power of our own inner light.

Kubera: Depicted as a stout green man hoisting a club to ensure justice, Kubera is the most prominent of the *yakshas*—the indigenous earth spirits of India. Known as the Protector of the World, he sits with his wife, Riddhi, the Journey of Life, atop his knee. As an embodiment of prosperity, in addition to Kubera's ever-present pot of gold, he often holds a ripe pomegranate to symbolize the fertility of our natural world.

The River Goddess: Dynamic energy and continuity, the River Goddess is water and fluidity, the power of flowing awareness and the imperative of movement. The current of fluids in our bodies creates health; the shift of our emotions demonstrates our humanity; our physical alterations from season to season, from year to year, illustrate our continual revivification, for to be alive is to change. The River Goddess personifies this essential force.

Sarasvati: This Goddess of All Things Creative exemplifies the power of imagination, the very spark of inspiration. Poetry, dance, painting—no matter what form art assumes, Sarasvati is the muse that ignites its personal expression. She is eloquence embodied.

Shiva/Lingam: Shiva symbolizes affirmation. He is life saying "Yes!" to life. As the dancing Nataraja, he illustrates the universe manifesting, the support of that creation, then its eventual dissolution as life shapes and reshapes itself again and again and again. He is the father of Ganapati and is often depicted in a family portrait that includes his beloved Uma as well as their second son, Murugan. As *lingam*, Shiva takes the Formless Form of latent possibility.

Shri: A cherry tree produces seeds in its fruit, a crow lays a pallid egg, a whale births a calf—all this is Shri, distributing the delight of life creating more life, and of that life thriving. Initiating all that is fecund, abundant, beautiful, and good, Shri is auspiciousness at its most generous. She is the glory of the evolutionary impetus, as the process of life itself expands into more.

Streak, the tiger: Streak plays the role of the illuminating energy of the deity Indra, whose weapon—the lightning bolt—hits its mark with precision and unmatched power. The illuminated mind does the same, lighting up our inner "sky" with clarity, as knowledge strikes like a brilliant thunderclap.

Together, the two cats Streak and ChiChi, represent the beauty of diversity in our friendships—the unlikely friends and allies we find in this world as we open ourselves to others. Mythically, Indra (Streak) and Soma (ChiChi) often act in tandem, as focus and impassioned effort together multiply their individual strengths.

Vishnu: Vishnu is sustenance: all the systems of stability, all the sources of perseverance. As the abiding in-dwelling light, Vishnu is awareness that consciousness is always at home within us. Simply by being born, we belong here.

The Map:

About the Author

With a lifelong involvement in Indian mythology and art history, author Hope West has worked closely with some of the world's most prestigious scholars in the field of South Asian studies. Inspired by her research, as well as her many pilgrimages to the great temple complexes of Tamil Nadu, this story is her story, a mythic tale that draws from her own insights to share the profound practices and wisdom offered by the uplifting philosophical traditions of the Sri Vidya of south India.

Printed in Canada